## 'I have seen y̶

Paige felt the b̶l̶ r̶ at his words.

'I don't want t̶o̶ ̶g̶o̶ ̶s̶w̶i̶mming,' she said, refusing to submit to his blackmail. 'I'd rather go back to the house.'

'It's cooler in the water,' remarked Nikolas softly, and she was irresistibly reminded of how soft the water would feel against her hot skin. Her hot, *bare* skin, she recalled, avoiding the dark sensuality of his muscled flesh. 'Have you become a prude?' he continued. 'Surely you know that no one but I can see you here?'

Paige breathed shallowly. 'That's not the point. I'm your employee. Not your guest.'

Nikolas lifted his shoulders. 'You would like to go swimming with me, but you're afraid of upsetting that stubborn little streak you call a conscience.'

'No! I just see no point in raking up the past. And besides, you're only having fun at my expense. What do you really want, Nikolas?'

**Anne Mather** has been writing since she was seven, but it was only when her first child was born that she fulfilled her dream of becoming a published author. Her first book, CAROLINE, met with immediate success and, since then, Anne has written more than 130 novels, reaching a readership which spans the world.

Born and raised in the north of England, Anne still makes her home there with her husband, two children and, now, grandchildren. Asked if she finds writing a lonely occupation, she replies that her characters always keep her company. In fact, she is so busy sorting out their lives that she often doesn't have time for her own! An avid reader herself, she devours everything from sagas and romances to suspense.

A *New York Times* bestselling author, Anne Mather has also seen one of her novels, LEOPARD IN THE SNOW, turned into a film.

**Recent titles by the same author:**

THE BABY GAMBIT
MORGAN'S CHILD

# THE MILLIONAIRE'S VIRGIN

BY
ANNE MATHER

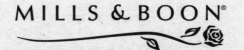

MILLS & BOON®

*First published in Great Britain 2000
Harlequin Mills & Boon Limited,
Eton House, 18-24 Paradise Road, Richmond, Surrey TW9 1SR*

© Anne Mather 2000

ISBN 0 263 81997 3

*Set in Times Roman 10½ on 11¼ pt.
01-0007-54519*

*Printed and bound in Spain
by Litografia Rosés, S.A., Barcelona*

# CHAPTER ONE

THE man sitting at the table wasn't Martin Price.

Paige's stomach hollowed and she glanced blankly at the waiter who was escorting her across the restaurant. There'd been some mistake. Martin's shoulders weren't as broad, his skin wasn't as dark, and his fair curls bore no resemblance to the thick black hair that erupted in rough splendour over the rim of white collar that was visible above his charcoal tailoring.

She was about to make her protest when the man rose to his feet and turned to face her. 'Ah, Paige,' he said, as her legs threatened to slip out from under her. 'How good of you to come.'

Paige didn't know what to do; what to say. There had been a mistake. She saw that now. And she'd made it. She'd believed she was coming here to meet her ex-fiancé, but it was obvious that that had only been a ploy on someone's part to get her here. She turned frantically to the waiter but he was already walking away, and although she badly wanted to follow him people were watching them and she was too much of a coward to make a scene.

'Won't you sit down?' he said, indicating the chair opposite. His lips parted in a thin smile. 'It's good to see you again.'

Paige hesitated. 'I don't understand.'

'You will.' His dark eyes narrowed between lashes that had always been absurdly long for a man. 'If you'll give me a few minutes of your time.'

'Why should I?' Paige was panicking now, but she couldn't help it.

'Oh, I think you owe me considerably more than that,'

5

he remarked, his expression hardening. 'Please—' It was hardly a request. 'Sit down.'

Paige drew in a breath but unless she wanted to embarrass herself she didn't have a lot of choice. Still, it was with evident reluctance that she subsided into the chair across the table, wrapping her hands about the purse in her lap as if it provided a lifeline.

'Good.' Having succeeded in his objective, he resumed his seat just as the wine waiter arrived at his elbow. 'Now, what will you have to drink?'

He was drinking wine, she noticed. Red wine that reflected the light from the chandeliers above their heads and gave off a ruby brilliance. She was tempted to join him; she loved wine and he knew it, but she had no intention of giving him any advantage and in her present condition it would probably go straight to her head.

'Um—just mineral water, please,' she murmured, after a moment, addressing herself to the waiter, and he gave her a polite little bow before going to attend to her order.

'Mineral water?' His tone was mocking now but Paige refused to be intimidated.

'What do you want, Nikolas?' she asked, avoiding his sardonic gaze. She didn't want to look into his eyes again, didn't want to feel the sudden rush of sexual awareness she'd felt when she'd first realised who he was. 'Where's Martin?'

'He's not coming.' He said the words without apology. 'Ah, here's your—water.'

Paige gazed at him now, ignoring the waiter completely. 'What do you mean, he's not coming?' she demanded. 'I think you'd better tell me what's going on.'

'Do you?' His tone was ironic. 'I gather he didn't explain the situation when he spoke to you.'

'No.'

Paige swallowed. She refused to admit that it was Martin's secretary who had contacted her and arranged this meeting. She'd been so relieved to hear from him again, she hadn't questioned why, after breaking their engagement, he'd suddenly decided to invite her to lunch at one of London's most exclusive restaurants. The fact that it used to be their favourite restaurant had persuaded her that Martin had had second thoughts and wanted to start seeing her again.

What a fool she'd been.

'So you have no idea why I invited you here?'

'Haven't I just said so?' Paige was abrupt, but she couldn't help it. This was just another occasion when nothing turned out as she'd expected.

'Tell me,' murmured Nikolas after a moment, his low, attractive voice barely exhibiting any trace of an accent, 'how long were you and Price—what shall I say?—' he frowned '—together?'

Paige stiffened. 'What business is that of yours?'

'Humour me.'

'Why should I?'

'Well...' He paused. 'If we are to have any kind of a working relationship—'

'A *what*!'

She interrupted him then, getting half out of her chair before his hand on her forearm pressed her down again into her seat. He did it so effortlessly, she thought, rubbing her arm when he released her, glaring at him with resentful eyes. All trace of sexual awareness was swamped now by the very real feelings of outrage that were gripping her.

'Calm down,' he said mildly. 'You are looking for a job, aren't you?' He regarded her dispassionately. 'I may have one to offer.'

'No, thanks.'

Paige looked away from his dark-skinned face, wondering how Martin could have done this to her. She'd thought he'd loved her. But she'd been wrong about that, too. Wrong about everything.

'Don't be too hasty,' Nikolas murmured now. He pushed the glass of water towards her. 'Drink. You'll feel better after some refreshment.'

'I don't want anything.' Paige realised she was behaving like a petulant child, but events were moving too fast for her to keep any kind of control over her emotions. She straightened her spine. 'I'd just like to know how Martin knew that you—that you and I—had—had—'

'Been lovers?' Nikolas suggested softly, and despite herself her face suffused with colour.

'Known one another,' she amended tersely. 'We were never lovers.'

'No.' He conceded the point with a certain amount of regret. 'Or you would not have done what you did, *ohi*?'

'I did nothing,' she insisted. 'Nothing wrong, that is.' Then, realising she was getting into deep waters, she added, 'How did Martin know we knew one another?'

'He didn't.' Nikolas was careless. 'As far as your— fiancé is concerned, we had never met before today.'

'He's not my fiancé.' Paige could feel her jaw quivering and hurriedly pressed her lips together to control it. 'I suppose you thought it was amusing, deceiving him like that?'

'I deceived no one.' His harsh features mirrored a momentary displeasure. 'Your Martin is not the most perceptive of men.'

'He's not my Martin.'

'No.' An air of satisfaction surrounded him at this admission. 'He told me that also.'

'He told you—' Paige's lips parted in dismay. 'He discussed our relationship with you.'

'Let us say that when your name entered the conversation I—persuaded him to confide in me,' declared Nikolas smugly. 'I can be very persuasive, as I'm sure you remember.'

Paige shook her head, refusing to explore that particular time bomb. 'What did he tell you? How do you know him?'

'Ah.' Nikolas relaxed back in his chair and Paige was reminded of a sleek predator that, having successfully subdued its prey, was now prepared to play with it. 'I happened to be looking for a new financial advisor and the firm of Seton Ross appeared to have an excellent reputation.'

'So you met quite by chance?'

'How else?'

She shook her head. 'I don't believe you.'

'Why not?' He adopted an air of injured innocence.

'Because if Nikolas Petronides approached a firm like Seton Ross he wouldn't be put off with one of the minor associates. Either Neville Ross or Andrew Dawes would have dealt with you personally.'

'Indeed.' Nikolas smiled. 'It pleases me that you would think I warrant a more expert evaluation than your—friend was able to offer. It proves that you have not been entirely deceived by his rather obvious charms. Be thankful he broke the engagement, *aghapita*. You can do much better, I am sure.'

Paige fumed. 'Don't patronise me.'

'Was I doing that?' Nikolas moved his silk-clad shoulders in a dismissive gesture. 'I am sorry.'

She was sure he was nothing of the kind, but she waited impatiently for him to go on. When he didn't, she said shortly, 'I'd still like to know how you came to discuss my—situation.'

'Yes...' He was evidently in no hurry to satisfy her curiosity. 'Well, let me see, how did the conversation go? I think we were discussing the recent fall in the stock market and how even recognised firms of stockbrokers were not immune from collapse. Naturally, Tennants was mentioned—'

'Naturally!'

'It was, after all, one of the most disastrous falls of the decade, was it not? And your father's untimely death was a real tragedy.' There was nothing but compassion in his face as he continued, 'Please: I cannot tell you how sorry I am; how much sympathy I feel for you and your sister.'

'We don't need your sympathy,' retorted Paige tightly, but even though it was months since her father had suffered the massive stroke that had ended his life she still felt totally bereft.

'*Etsi ki alios*, it is sincere,' Nikolas assured her. 'Although I had no love for the man, I would not wish what happened to him on my worst enemy.'

Paige regarded him coldly. 'So you decided to offer me a job,' she said scornfully. 'How kind!'

'Do not be bitter, Paige.' Nikolas sighed. 'It does not become you. Just because your fiancé has deserted you, do not—'

'How dare you?'

Once again, Paige attempted to push her chair away from the table, but this time the waiter thwarted her. Misunderstanding, he assumed she was trying to pull her chair closer to the table, and he assisted her in doing just that before presenting her with the menu.

'I'll be back in a few minutes to take your order,' he said politely, and Paige was obliged to stay where she was, at least until he had returned to his station.

But as soon as he'd moved away she fixed Nikolas with a furious stare. 'How dare you?' she demanded again. 'How dare you discuss my private life with—with—?'

'With the man you'd hoped to share your life with?' suggested her companion drily. 'Perhaps you should be asking him why he's telling all and sundry that the Tennant sisters are virtually penniless.'

'Oh, I intend to.'

'What?' Nikolas's brows rose sardonically. 'And give him the satisfaction of knowing how much he's hurt you? Think again, Paige. As I said before, he's not worth it.'

'And you are?' She was contemptuous.

'Let us say, I have reason to enjoy your humiliation. He does not.'

Paige glanced about her. 'And that's what this is all about? Humiliation?'

'No.'

'Oh, please…' She gazed at him disbelievingly. 'At least have the decency to tell me the truth.'

'I will. If you'll let me.' He shrugged. 'Have lunch with me. That is why you came, after all.'

'To have lunch with Martin,' she corrected him tersely, and then, remembering what her ex-fiancé had done, she realised how pathetic that sounded. She hesitated. 'Why should I?'

'Because you're here; because you're curious.' His thin lips twitched. 'Let me tell you why I let Price arrange this meeting.'

Paige took a considering breath but once again the waiter made the decision for her. Returning to take their order, he regarded them both with polite, enquiring eyes, and Nikolas turned somewhat impatiently to his own menu.

'Shall I order for us both?' he enquired, and because Paige was too bemused to argue with him she gave an unwilling nod. 'We'll have the avocado mousse and the grilled salmon,' he told the waiter smoothly. 'It is fresh salmon, not farmed?' After gaining the waiter's reassurance, he said, 'Thank you.'

Paige had forgotten how efficient Nikolas was in any situation. How easily he could make a decision and act on it without resorting to discussion. He could decide what he was going to eat in less time than it had taken Martin to open a menu, and he had an effortless air of command that would persuade even the hardiest *maître d'* to do his bidding.

The waiter collected the menus and went away and they were alone again. But not for long. The wine waiter returned with his list, but this time Nikolas was ready for him. 'A bottle of the '97 Chardonnay,' he said, waving the list away. 'That's all.'

Paige breathed deeply, trying desperately to achieve even a little of his composure, but it was almost impossible. Despite her frustration at being put in such a position, she couldn't deny a certain exhilaration at this unexpected turn of events. It was a long time since anything had inspired her to the kind of emotional upheaval Nikolas had so effortlessly created. And, while she still resented the way both he and Martin had treated her, her eyes were continually drawn to the lean brown fingers that played with the stem of his glass and the coarse black hair that dusted his wrists below the pristine cuffs of his shirt.

Nikolas was such a masculine animal, she thought, a sense of suffocation at his nearness almost overwhelming her. The only man she'd ever known who could reduce her to trembling supplication with just a single look. Or, at least, he had when she was younger, she corrected herself fiercely. She was much older—much wiser—now.

'So,' he said, startling her out of her reverie, 'you would like to know about the job, *ne*?'

'If I must,' she answered tautly. 'If there really is a job.'

'You think I would be here otherwise?'

Paige realised that to admit that that was what she had been thinking was conceited, and amended her response. 'Perhaps.'

'First of all, am I right in assuming that you are looking for employment?' he asked softly, and two red flags of colour burned in her pale cheeks.

'If Martin said it, then it must be true,' she replied frostily, resenting the question. 'I suppose he also told you I have no qualifications to speak of.'

'You have discussed your problems with him?' Nikolas frowned.

'No.' Paige was indignant. 'Sophie did. She's desperate for me to get a job so we can find somewhere else to live.'

'Ah, Sophie.' He nodded. 'Your sister. Regrettably, we were never introduced.'

Paige shrugged. 'She was at school when—when—'

'When your father was attempting to blind me with his elder daughter's beauty?' suggested Nikolas ironically. 'Yes, I know. How old is she now?'

'Sixteen.' Paige pursed her lips. And then, because she couldn't let him get away with defaming her father's memory, she added, 'And Daddy only introduced us. It wasn't his fault that we—that you betrayed his trust.'

Nikolas's lips twisted. 'You do not really believe that.'

'Why not? And the Murchison deal appeared to be an attractive proposition. He was trying to do you a favour by offering you the chance to invest…'

'In something that folded only a few months later,' remarked her companion bleakly. 'At which time, I'd have lost a considerable amount of money.'

*You could afford it,* thought Paige defiantly, but she kept that opinion to herself. 'It might have succeeded if you'd been prepared to back it,' she said instead, only to meet a blank wall of contempt.

'Be honest,' said Nikolas harshly. '*Theos*, the shipping line was already losing money and all your father really wanted was someone else to share the burden of his mistake. Why else do you think he destroyed our relationship? As soon as he realised he was wasting his time with me, he moved on to the next—what is that word you use?—sucker? Yes, sucker.'

'That's not true.'

'Of course it's true.'

'No—'

'Yes—'

'Avocado mousse, madam.'

The arrival of the meal put an end to any further argument, and although Paige had the feeling she was betraying her father's memory by even being here now she refused to let Nikolas Petronides have the last word. All the same, meeting his dark eyes across the table, eyes that could turn from black velvet to burnished agate in a twinkling, she suspected she was playing a dangerous game.

'Perhaps we should discuss why I had Price invite you here,' he declared, after the waiter had departed again. 'I'm sure you understand why I prevailed upon him to offer the invitation. I was fairly sure that were I to contact you you would not submit.'

'Submit?' Paige pushed the delicate mousse around her plate. 'That's a typically Petronides word to use, isn't it? But you're right. I wouldn't have come.'

'I thought not.' He paused. 'That was why I suggested that as Price was a friend of yours he should arrange this meeting.'

Paige absorbed this as the wine waiter poured some of the deliciously flavoured Chardonnay into her glass. But when they were alone again she exclaimed, 'And Martin had no idea that—that we knew one another?'

'I'm afraid not.' Nikolas looked at her over the rim of his own glass. 'Poor Paige. The men in your life do seem perfectly willing to throw you to the—wolves, do they not?'

Paige refused to let him provoke her. 'Is that a warning, Kirie Petronides?' she asked mockingly, and had the satisfaction of seeing his eyes darken accordingly.

But, 'Maybe,' was all he said, and it was Paige who felt every nerve in her body tingle at the veiled menace in his voice.

They didn't speak again until the grilled salmon had been served and then it was Paige who felt compelled to break the uneasy silence that had fallen. 'I—I would have expected Yanis to handle any employee recruitment,' she murmured, aware that she had barely touched the mousse and was only making a paltry effort with the salmon. A morsel caught in her dry throat and she was forced to cough and resort to her wine before continuing, 'He is still with you, I assume?'

Nikolas was not deceived by her attempt at casual conversation. 'Yanis is still my assistant, *ne*,' he conceded evenly. 'But this is a rather—delicate affair.'

'Why?' Despite herself, Paige was puzzled. She couldn't believe it was anything to do with her.

'Because it is a personal matter,' he replied, taking another mouthful of his wine. Then, because she was still looking at him enquiringly, he went on, 'The job I have in mind concerns my ward. In such circumstances, it is not— suitable—to leave the decision in Yanis's hands.'

Paige gasped. 'Your ward?' She looked stunned. 'I didn't know you had a ward.'

'That is because I did not have a ward when we—knew one another,' he told her. 'Ariadne's father was a close friend, and when he and his wife were killed three years ago I discovered they had appointed me their daughter's guardian. She has no other close relatives, you understand? *Oriste*, I have a ward.'

'I see.' Paige moved her shoulders uncertainly. 'That's quite a responsibility. How old is she?'

'Ariadne is seventeen years of age. Not too much of a responsibility, as you can see.'

'Oh.' Paige was surprised. 'Then why—?'

'I am looking for a young woman of good family to— how shall I put it?—keep her company for the summer. And to share with her all those womanly confidences she can no longer share with her mother.'

'And you thought that I—?'

'In the absence of any other offers, yes,' he essayed mildly. 'Why not?'

Paige gasped. 'I couldn't work for you.'

'Do not be too hasty, *aghapita*.' He speared her with a penetrating look. 'The position carries a generous salary with all expenses found, and the hours would not be too arduous.'

'I'm not for sale, Nikolas.'

'No, but you are short of funds, are you not? And you said yourself that your sister is eager for you to find alternative accommodation, *ne*?'

Paige put down her fork. 'This is a pointless conversation. I don't speak Greek.'

'Ariadne understands English. She is still at school, of course. But she has been educated to a very high standard.'

'Then she's probably perfectly capable of taking care of herself,' said Paige, thinking of her own sister. Sophie would die if anyone suggested she needed a chaperon. 'Besides, as you've just mentioned, I have a sister, who— who—' *Had been quite a handful since Paige had had to remove her from the expensive boarding school she'd been attending.* 'Who I couldn't possibly leave on her own.'

Or with Aunt Ingrid, she appended ruefully. Ever since their father died, they'd been staying with their mother's sister in her 'bijou' cottage, as she described it, in Islington. And it was only because Paige was there to keep the peace between them that Sophie and her aunt remained on speaking terms…

'Then bring her with you,' said Nikolas carelessly. 'She will be on holiday, too, will she not? And I would prefer Ariadne to stay at my house on Skiapolis for the summer.' He shrugged. 'There is plenty of room, as you know, and your sister may befriend Ariadne. They are of a similar age.'

They were, but Paige could imagine Sophie's reaction were she to drop this particular bombshell in her lap. Although her sister resented the circumstances in which they were now being forced to live, blaming their father for not making adequate provision for them during his lifetime, she would find the idea of leaving London for some unsophisticated island in the Aegean even more unacceptable. Besides, she'd just settled down at the local comprehensive; she'd made friends; and although Paige wasn't altogether enthusiastic about the crowd Sophie was mixing with she had no desire to uproot her again.

'I don't think so,' she said now, bestowing a slightly warmer smile on the waiter when he came to remove her barely touched plate. 'No, it was fine,' she assured him when he expressed his concern. Then, looking at Nikolas again, she said, 'I'm afraid you've wasted your time.'

'No time is ever wasted,' he responded, his brooding expression giving the lie to his words. 'At least think about it, Paige. I shall be in London for a few more days and you can always contact me via this number.' He drew out a card and scrawled some figures on the back before pushing it across the table towards her. 'Take it.'

Somewhat against her better judgement, Paige reached for the card, but as she did so Nikolas covered her hand with his, successfully imprisoning her fingers within his cool grasp. And, although she made a futile attempt to free herself, she knew she had no real chance of competing with his strength.

'Think about it. Please,' he begged softly, and Paige was overwhelmed by the sensual appeal in his voice.

Dear God, she thought, dragging her eyes away from his to gaze unsteadily at the powerful fist encasing hers. A fiery warmth was spreading up her arm and invading every quivering pore of her slender frame, and no matter how she tried to rationalise her reaction she knew her body hadn't forgotten anything about this man. It remembered; her *skin* remembered; and that was something she had never expected.

Eventually, he was obliged to let her draw her hand away and she cradled it in her lap, as if it had been abused. That was what it felt like, she thought shakily, the vibration his touch had evoked still rippling through her veins. She just prayed he wasn't aware of her upheaval.

Somehow she got through the next few minutes. Although she didn't want it, she agreed to coffee in lieu of a pudding, and endeavoured to come to terms with the fact that she had more than one reason for refusing his offer. Even if it was the only offer that came her way, she couldn't work for him. Apart from anything else, she didn't want to be hurt again, and Nikolas Petronides would have no qualms about recovering what he saw as his pound of flesh…

## CHAPTER TWO

PAIGE caught the Underground back to Islington. At this time of the afternoon, the trains weren't busy, and after finding herself a seat she reflected how quickly she'd adapted to using the Tube instead of taking taxis everywhere.

All the same, it had been raining when she'd left the restaurant, and she'd had to resist Nikolas's offer to get a taxi for her. Although it was June, the weather was still unseasonably cold, and the pretty cream Chanel suit she'd worn to impress Martin was now dotted with damp patches.

She just hoped it didn't pick up any dirt on the way home. She and Sophie were having to conserve what clothes they had, and it had been quite a drain on their meagre resources outfitting her sister with clothes for her new school.

She sighed. If only their father were still alive, she thought wistfully, but Parker Tennant had died as he'd lived: without making any provision for the future. He'd left his daughters with a mountain of debt besides, and the unhappy task of having to salvage what little they could from his possessions. Not that there had been much. The beautiful home they'd had in Surrey had been mortgaged twice over, and even their mother's jewels had had to be sold to satisfy their creditors.

Paige thought it was just as well their mother hadn't lived to see it. Annabel Tennant had died of an obscure form of cancer when Paige was seventeen and Sophie only ten, and she'd sometimes wondered whether that was when her father had started taking such enormous risks with his clients' money. It was as if his wife's death had persuaded him that there was no point in planning for a future that might never happen, and there was no doubt that losing her mother had affected him badly.

It was why Paige had left school without finishing her education; why she'd appointed herself his protector. She'd been there when he needed her, taking care of him when he didn't, and somehow getting him through those first awful months after Annabel died.

It had taken a toll on her, too, but she'd never considered herself. She'd been happy making him happy, and until she'd been introduced to Nikolas Petronides she'd cared little for the fact that the only men she'd dated had been men her father had had dealings with.

Of course, he'd approved of Nikolas, too—at least to begin with. It was only when he'd discovered that the Greek had had no intention of investing money with him that he'd turned against him. And Paige had had no doubts where her loyalties lay...

Which was why there was no way she could accept Nikolas's offer now. Apart from the fact that they had once known one another too well, she wanted nothing from him. In his own way, he was like Martin: he was using her situation to humiliate her, and however attractive the prospect of a summer in Greece might be—not to mention the generous salary he'd tried to bribe her with—she needed a real job with someone who wasn't out for revenge.

But she didn't want to think about that now. It was four years since her relationship with Nikolas had foundered and since then she'd insisted on taking charge of her own life. She sighed. Not that she'd been any more successful, she conceded wryly. Her association with Martin Price had hardly been a success. But then, she hadn't been aware that the handsome young accountant had been more interested in furthering his own career, and in paying court to Parker Tennant's daughter he had envisaged a partnership in her father's investment brokerage firm as his reward. Of course, when Parker Tennant died in such inauspicious circumstances, he'd quickly amended his plans. In a very short time, Paige had found her engagement had only been as secure as her father's bank balance, and although Martin had made some excuse about finding someone else she'd known exactly what he really meant.

She stared dully out of the window. That was why she'd felt so mortified when she'd learned that Martin had arranged for her to see Nikolas Petronides. It was galling to think that his prime concern was to put some distance between them, and she half wished she could tell him exactly what she and Nikolas had once been to one another. Would he be jealous? She doubted it. Of Nikolas's wealth, perhaps, but nothing else.

The train pulled into her station and, leaving her seat, she discovered to her relief that it had stopped raining. Which was just as well, as she had a ten-minute walk to Claremont Avenue, and no umbrella.

Aunt Ingrid's cottage was about halfway down the avenue, and Paige approached the house with some relief. It had been quite a day, one way and another, and she was looking forward to changing into shorts and a T-shirt and spending some time weeding her aunt's pocket-sized garden. It was what she needed, she thought: mindless physical exercise, with nothing more momentous to think about than what the soil was doing to her nails.

She heard her aunt's and her sister's voices before she'd even opened the front gate. The windows of the cottage were open and their raised tones rang with unpleasantly familiar resonance on the still air. Several of her aunt's neighbours were taking advantage of the break in the weather to catch up on outdoor jobs, and they could hear them, too, and Paige offered the elderly couple next door an apologetic smile as she hurried up the path.

What now? she wondered wearily. She glanced at her

watch. It was barely three o'clock. Sophie shouldn't even be home from school yet. For heaven's sake, didn't she have enough to worry about as it was?

'You're a selfish, stupid girl,' Aunt Ingrid was saying angrily as Paige let herself into the house.

'And you're a harried old bag,' retorted Sophie, before there was the ominous sound of flesh meeting flesh. There was a howl from her sister before she apparently responded in kind, and Paige slammed the door and charged across the tiny hall and into the over-furnished parlour just as her aunt was collapsing into a Regency-striped love-seat, her hand pressed disbelievingly to her cheek.

'For goodness' sake!' Paige stared at them incredulously. 'What on earth is going on? I could hear you when I turned into the avenue.'

That was an exaggeration, but they were not to know that, and it had the effect of bringing a groan of anguish from her aunt. The thought that someone else might have been a party to her disgrace was too much, and Paige, who had been hoping to shame her sister, gave a resigned sigh.

Of course, Sophie was unlikely to care what anyone else thought, and as if to prove this she would have pushed past her sister and left the room if Paige hadn't grabbed her arm. 'Where do you think you're going?' she demanded. 'I asked what was going on here. You might as well tell me. I'm going to find out anyway. Have you been excluded from school? What?'

'Ask her.' Sophie's face was mutinous. She gave her aunt a baleful look. 'She's the one who's been poking around in my things.'

Paige didn't make the mistake of letting go of her arm. 'I asked you,' she reminded her shortly, although her heart sank at the thought that Sophie might have some justification for her complaint. Casting a silent appeal in the older woman's direction, she added, 'This is Aunt Ingrid's house, not yours.'

'Ask her what she's got hidden in her underwear drawer.'

Aunt Ingrid's voice was frail and unsteady, and for a moment Paige wanted to smile. Dear God, what had Sophie been hiding? See-through bras; sexy knickers; what? Then, the reluctant admission that Ingrid shouldn't have been looking through Sophie's belongings anyway wiped the embryo grin of amusement off her face.

'Yeah, how about that?' Sophie broke in before she could respond. 'The old bat's been prying into my drawers, in more ways than one. Nosy old bitch! I told you that we had no privacy here—'

'She's a drug addict, Paige.' The older woman's voice trembled now. 'An addict, in my house. I never thought I'd live to see the day that my own sister's child—'

'What is Aunt Ingrid talking about?' Despite the fact that the old lady had been known to exaggerate at times, her words had struck a chill into Paige's bones. 'Why should she say you're a drug addict?'

'She's lying—'

'No, I'm not.'

'She is,' insisted Sophie scornfully. 'She doesn't know what she's talking about.' She gave a short laugh. 'I'm not an addict. For God's sake, I doubt if she'd know one if she saw one.'

'I know what marijuana smells like,' retorted her aunt tremulously. 'You're not the first generation to discover illegal substances, you know.'

'So?' Sophie sneered. 'You're no better than me.'

'I didn't use heroin!' exclaimed Aunt Ingrid, with evident disgust, and Paige's jaw dropped.

'Heroin?' she echoed weakly, turning to stare at her sister. 'Oh, Sophie, is this true? Have you been using heroin?'

'No—'

'Then what was it doing in your drawer?' demanded her aunt, and Paige endorsed her question.

'Oh, I should have known that you'd take her side,' muttered Sophie sulkily, without answering. 'Whatever I say now, you're not going to believe me.'

'Try me.'

'You don't have to take my word for it,' persisted the old lady. 'Go into your bedroom, Paige. You can smell it for yourself. Marijuana has a most distinctive scent: sweet and very heady. That was why I looked though Sophie's belongings. I was expecting to find a pack of joints.'

Paige shook her head. 'I wouldn't recognise marijuana, Aunt Ingrid. It may sound stupid, but I've never smoked a joint in my life.' She frowned. 'But I thought you said you found heroin in the drawer?'

'I did.'

Sophie snorted. 'She has no right to criticise me. She's obviously familiar with drugs or she wouldn't be accusing me.'

Paige caught her breath. 'You admit that you've been smoking marijuana?' she exclaimed, horrified, and Sophie gave her a pitying look.

'Where have you been living for the past ten years, Paige?' she exhorted. 'Not on this planet!'

'Don't you dare try and justify it,' cried her aunt, but Sophie wasn't listening to her.

'Everyone uses these days,' she said, and Paige stared at her with disbelieving eyes.

'I don't,' she said, but somehow that wasn't enough.

A sense of panic gripped her. What was she going to do now? When she'd accepted responsibility for Sophie, she'd never expected anything like this.

Her aunt shifted in her chair. 'Aren't you forgetting something, Paige?' she asked. Then, after fumbling in the pocket of her trousers, she declared, 'This.'

'This' was a tiny plastic packet of white powder and Paige could only guess at what it was. 'Oh, Sophie,' she exclaimed, feeling sick to her stomach. 'Where did you get it? What is it doing in your drawer?'

Sophie hunched her shoulders. 'That's my business.'

'Not as long as you're living in my house, young lady,' retorted her aunt sharply, and Paige wanted to groan aloud when her sister answered back.

'We won't be living in your house much longer,' she announced triumphantly. 'Paige is going to find us a decent place of our own, aren't you, Paige? Somewhere better than this shoebox, without any crazy old woman telling us how to live our lives.'

'Sophie—'

Paige's protest was useless. There was only so much their aunt would take, she knew that, and Sophie had tried her patience for the last time. Struggling to her feet, she pointed a trembling finger at the younger girl. 'That's it,' she said. 'I've had enough of you and your insolence. I don't care what Paige does, but I want you out of here tonight!'

Two weeks later, Paige stood at the window of their room in the small bed-and-breakfast, watching somewhat anxiously for the taxi that was going to take them to the airport. It was already fifteen minutes late and her palms were damp with the realisation that if they missed the flight they would also miss the ferry that would take them to Skiapolis.

Behind her, Sophie lounged sulkily on her bed, making no attempt to gather her belongings together. She had left her sister to do all their packing, and Paige had had to bite her tongue against the urge to tell Sophie that this was all her fault. But it was. And Paige could have done with some reassurance that she wasn't making yet another mistake.

Glancing round, she met the younger girl's defiant gaze with some impatience. If only Sophie were older: if only she could have been relied upon to pull her weight, they might have got through this. Aunt Ingrid wasn't a monster. With a little persuasion on Sophie's part, the older woman would have come round.

As it was, with no other job in prospect and bills to pay, Paige had been compelled to call the number Nikolas Petronides had given her. At least working for him would give her a breathing space, she'd consoled herself, and if she saved every penny he paid her there might be enough to put the deposit down on a small apartment by the time they came back to England.

It had been a relief to find that someone other than Nikolas had answered when she'd rung. A man, who had introduced himself as Donald Jamieson, and who was apparently Nikolas's solicitor, had been left to handle the details. He'd explained that Mr Petronides had had to return to Greece, but he'd issued instructions to the effect that if Paige should decide to take the job Jamieson should make the necessary arrangements for their journey.

Although she'd been reassured by Jamieson's involvement Paige had wondered briefly if she was being entirely wise in accepting the position. It was useless telling herself that Nikolas couldn't possibly have known she'd change her mind. That the instructions he'd left had been a logical attempt to cover all eventualities. But the fact was, Nikolas was an arrogant devil, and had it not been for Sophie's problems she'd have done almost anything rather than accept his help.

Still, she consoled herself, it was only for the summer, and a lot of things could change in three months. Aunt Ingrid had been horrified when she'd explained what they were planning to do. As far as she was concerned, Paige was jeopardising her own future for the sake of a girl who had no appreciation of the fact. And, because the Petronides name meant nothing more to her than the logo on the side of an oil tanker, she'd considered Paige's decision reckless in the extreme.

Which hadn't improved her relationship with Sophie one iota. The younger girl continued to assert that despite the presence of the heroin in her drawer she'd never actually touched hard drugs, but Paige had known she couldn't trust her not to use them in the future. She'd been horrified to learn that Sophie's introduction to marijuana wasn't a recent thing either. According to her, it had been in common use at her boarding-school, but if she'd thought that might reassure her sister she couldn't have been more wrong. Paige had been appalled, and more convinced than ever that she was doing the right thing by getting Sophie out of London.

She scanned the street again for the mini-cab that had promised to pick them up twenty minutes ago. She hoped it came soon. In spite of everything, she didn't want to admit that she was getting cold feet.

'Come on, come on,' she muttered impatiently, and Sophie, who had been viewing her sister's agitation with a certain amount of satisfaction, now sat up. Pushing back the crinkled shoulder-length perm that was several shades lighter than Paige's toffee-streaked blonde hair, she looked more optimistic than she'd done since Paige had first told her that she was going to accept the job in Greece.

'Does this mean we're going to miss the plane?' she asked smugly, and Paige knew exactly how her aunt must have felt when she'd confronted Sophie's insolent stare.

'No,' she retorted at once, although she wasn't absolutely sure what she'd do if they did miss the flight. After all, it was the holiday season. Flights were booked well in advance. 'We'll just take a later plane,' she added shortly, 'so you might as well resign yourself to the fact that we're going to Skiapolis.'

'Skiapolis!' Sophie spoke disparagingly. 'It wouldn't be so bad if it was Athens, or Rhodes, even. Somewhere I'd heard of. But Skiapolis! I don't know how you can even justify what you're doing to me. If Daddy was alive, he'd—'

She broke off, and Paige seized her chance. 'Yes?' she prompted. 'If Daddy was alive—what? What would he do?

Do you think he'd be proud to learn that his younger daughter was a—a junkie?'

Sophie sniffed. 'I'm not a junkie.'

'So you say.' Paige was scornful now. 'And what about what you did to Aunt Ingrid? Daddy was very fond of Aunt Ingrid. Do you think he'd applaud you for beating her up?'

'I didn't beat her up.' Sophie was indignant. 'She slapped me first.'

'There are other ways of beating up old people than by hitting them,' retorted Paige without hesitation. 'What if she'd had a seizure? How would you have felt then?'

Sophie's shoulders hunched. 'She'd been nosing about in my things. She had no right to do that.'

'And you had no right to sneak out of school before your last period,' Paige reminded her sharply. 'If you'd had nothing to hide, we wouldn't even be having this conversation.'

'I wish we weren't.'

'I dare say you do. But we are, and that's all there is to it.' Paige heard the unmistakable sound of a car in the cul-de-sac outside and breathed a sigh of relief. 'Here's the taxi. Grab your things. We're leaving.'

Sophie flounced off the bed. 'I'll never forgive you for this, Paige. Never! Forcing me to go and live on some grotty old Greek island with some grotty old business acquaintance of Daddy's. I'm going to be bored out of my mind.'

'Better bored than stoned,' replied Paige tersely, wishing she felt more positive. And at least Sophie knew nothing about Nikolas, other than the story she'd invented about how she'd got the job. In fact, she'd left Sophie with the impression that if she hadn't gone crying to Martin about their problems Paige might never have been offered the position at all.

It was late afternoon when they arrived in Athens and the heat was palpable. Even Sophie breathed a little sigh of wonder as they walked down the steps off the plane. With the sun striking on the airport buildings, reflecting back off the glass, and heat rising up from the tarmac, the unaccustomed brilliance was dazzling. For a few minutes, even Sophie forgot her complaints as they walked the short distance to the arrivals hall.

The formalities were soon dealt with. The Greek officials were not immune to the attractions of two young women travelling alone, and in a very short time their luggage was stowed in the boot of an ancient cab, and they were on their way to Piraeus. The ferry was due to depart at seven o'clock that evening, and Paige was hoping they might have time to grab a bite to eat before they boarded the ship. She had no idea what facilities might be provided on the vessel. Her own trips to Greece with her father had never entailed travelling between the mainland and the many islands that dotted the area. Of course, they had visited Skiapolis—but that had been as guests aboard Nikolas's yacht. This was an entirely different situation, and she had no illusions about the position she now occupied in his life.

Piraeus was the largest and busiest port in Greece. Ferries ran from its harbour to most of the larger islands in the Greek archipelago, some of the bigger ones looking as luxurious as cruise ships.

Paige doubted that the ferry to Skiapolis would fall into that category. Her memory was that it had been one of the smaller islands in the group. Nikolas owned most, if not all, of the island, and he hadn't wanted to encourage tourists, at least in those days. A small ferry had brought mail and essential supplies, she remembered, but she doubted it possessed tourist accommodation. She was grateful the trip wasn't a long one. They might have been obliged to sleep on deck.

The instructions they'd been given obliged them to collect their tickets from an agent at the Plateia Karaiskaki, and after the car had dropped them off they carried their bags across the busy concourse. Sophie was briefly stunned by the heat and the smells and the alien language, but although she exclaimed at the brilliance of the sea she was beginning to find the late afternoon sun more of a burden than a blessing. She grumbled every time someone jostled her, or the strap of her rucksack dug into her shoulder.

They eventually found the office they were looking for. Paige went to see about their tickets and was given the number of the quay where the ferry was supposed to leave from. But she was also informed that a seven o'clock departure schedule meant very little. If the ferry was late arriving at the port, they could be looking at nine o'clock or later.

Sophie understood little of the conversation Paige was having with the agent. The office was hot and stuffy, and she was quite happy to spend her time guarding their luggage beside the open door. And exchanging provocative glances with a curly-headed youth in jeans and trainers, whose brown, sun-bronzed arms were seen to advantage in his sleeveless T-shirt.

Their silent flirtation had not gone unnoticed, however. Paige, trying to concentrate on what the agent was saying, made furious gestures at her sister, but without much success. Hot and frustrated, Paige was beginning to wish they'd never left London. At least in England she could understand what was going on.

With the tickets in her hand, she eventually escaped the counter and pushed her way across to where Sophie was waiting. The youth was chatting her up now and, judging by the becoming flush in Sophie's cheeks, she was having no trouble understanding him. Indeed, she hardly noticed Paige's arrival, her husky laugh attracting the attention of more than one pair of eyes.

'Sophie!' Paige dug her in the ribs with her elbow, bending to pick up her own bags before confronting her sister with a baleful look. 'Come on,' she said, ignoring the boy. 'Let's go and find a café. I'm dying for a cool drink.'

'Wait a minute.' Sophie grabbed her arm, and although Paige prepared herself for an argument it didn't come. 'This is Paris,' she said, as if that was of some interest to them. 'Mr Petronides has sent him to meet us. Isn't that great?'

Paige blinked. 'What?'

'Kirie Petronides,' ventured the young man helpfully. 'You are Kiria Tennant, *ohi*? And Thespinis Tennant,' he added, smiling at Sophie. '*Kalostone, kiria.* Welcome to Greece.'

Paige dropped her bags again. 'Kirie Petronides asked you to meet us?' she asked disbelievingly, even as the boy's distinction between greeting an older woman and a younger one caused her to grit her teeth. Still, she probably looked a lot older, she conceded, right at this moment. She was hot and tired, and she wasn't in the mood for precocious youths.

'*Ne,*' he said, looping the strap of Sophie's rucksack over his shoulder and picking up her suitcase without obvious effort. 'If you will come with me…'

'Wait.' Paige hesitated. 'How do I know—?' she began, only to have Sophie override her protests.

'Come on, Paige,' she muttered in a low voice. 'How else did he know our names?'

'Perhaps he heard me speaking to the ticket agent,' replied Paige uneasily. And then, realising she hadn't mentioned Nikolas's name, she muttered, 'Oh—all right.'

But she wasn't about to stagger across the quay again with both her bags. If the boy could carry one suitcase so easily, he could carry two. Tapping him on the arm, she gestured towards the other bag, and although his smile slipped a little he nodded and picked it up.

'Isn't he a babe?' Sophie whispered as they followed his sinuous saunter away from the busy ferry terminal and along a narrow quay where private yachts and motor vessels bobbed on the rising swell. 'Great buns!'

'Sophie!' Paige realised she sounded like an old maid, but her sister's language was too liberally peppered with comments of that kind. 'You watch too much television.'

'Well, I won't be watching it from now on, will I?' Sophie retorted, and Paige didn't know if that was a blessing or not. When she'd insisted on them coming out here, she hadn't considered that there might be other distractions, and Paris—if that was his name—might be far too available.

Still, she couldn't worry about that now. This was their first real introduction to the blue waters of the Aegean, and the breeze blowing off the water was refreshingly cool against Paige's hot cheeks.

By the time they reached their transport, a steady trickle of perspiration was dampening the skin between her breasts and the hair on the back of her neck was wet. Although she'd warned Sophie against wearing anything skimpy to travel in, she was wishing she hadn't taken her own advice now. The denim skirt and matching waistcoat, worn over a simple round-necked navy blue T-shirt, had seemed perfectly suitable when they'd boarded the plane in London. Now, however, the shirt was sticking to her, and she wished she'd taken the time to go into the restroom at the airport and remove the white tights that were cutting into her legs.

Sophie looked hot, too, but she'd pulled her shirt out of her cropped jeans and tied it beneath her breasts. Paige hadn't had the heart to stop her, even though she knew no Greek girl would dress that way. Well, no Greek girl of Nikolas's family, she amended, thinking of Ariadne. But if Nikolas didn't like it he had only himself to blame.

The vessel that awaited them was not a yacht. Paige, who had briefly entertained the thought that Nikolas himself might have come to meet them, quickly revised her opinion. The sleek motor launch was much smaller than the other vessel and it was deserted, its fringed canopy flapping in the breeze. But at least it would provide some protection, she thought gratefully. She couldn't wait to get out of the sun.

Paris threw their bags onto the deck and then jumped aboard. Paige felt a momentary twinge of irritation at his treatment of their luggage and then decided it was probably no worse than the handling they'd suffered on the plane. He held out his hand to Sophie, and she quickly followed after him. Then he did the same for Paige, taking a good look at her white-clad thighs as her skirt lifted in the breeze.

He grinned then, aware of her indignation, and although she wanted to be cross with him she found herself smiling, too. He was only a boy, she told herself as he took her suitcase from her and stowed it with the rest of the luggage in the steering cabin. He probably lived and worked on the island, and they were unlikely to see him again.

# CHAPTER THREE

PAIGE regarded her reflection in the long mirrored doors of
the closet and wondered why she was taking so much trouble over her appearance tonight. It wasn't as if she wanted
to impress anyone; not with her looks anyway. But she was
nervous about meeting Ariadne for the first time and finding
out if they were likely to get along.

She had wondered if the girl would be curious to meet
them but evidently Ariadne did not regard paid companions
as honoured guests. Instead, it had been left to a black-
garbed housekeeper to greet the new arrivals, and although
Paige thought she was vaguely familiar Kiria Papandreiu
had given no indication that they had met before.

The journey to the island had not been unpleasant,
though it had taken rather longer than Paige remembered.
Still, once they were out of the busy harbour, Paris had
provided light refreshments, and because she'd eaten little
of the lunch on the plane Paige was grateful for his consideration.

So much so that she hadn't objected when Sophie had
asked if she could go up front with Paris. Of course she
hadn't anticipated that Sophie would spend most of the
journey seated beside him at the controls. But having given
her permission there was little she could do about it and at
least it had kept her sister occupied throughout the two-
hour trip.

Arriving at the small port of Agios Petros had been rather
nerve-racking. It had been dark, and although Paige hadn't
expected anyone to meet them at the quay she had anticipated that Nikolas would be waiting at the house. But she'd
been wrong. When they'd emerged from the car that had

34

brought them up from the harbour, Kiria Papandreiu had explained, albeit in barely comprehensible English, that Kirie Petronides was away. Where he was, she didn't say; nor when he'd be back. But, once again, Paige got the impression that as employees they didn't warrant that kind of information.

It was all a far cry from the last time she was here, she reflected wistfully, and then chided herself for allowing thoughts of that kind to colour her mood. She'd been a guest then, not a servant, and Nikolas had done his best to make both her and her father welcome.

But Parker Tennant hadn't known what was really going on...

She stiffened now, smoothing down the calf-length skirt of her turquoise taffeta sheath. She'd hesitated some time before choosing the fairly formal outfit, but until she knew what was expected of her, she'd rather not take any chances. However, the clothes she'd bought for the trip, both for her and Sophie, had been off the peg. Sophie, who had grown in the last year, had needed a selection of summer clothes, but Paige herself had had to make do with a couple of dresses.

Fortunately her hair was easy to handle. Unlike Sophie's, she wore it fairly short and straight, the simple bob curling under at her chin. When she'd known Nikolas before, her hair had been long and she'd worn it in a French braid, but that was in the days when a visit to the hairdressers' was a weekly event.

She sighed, touching her hot cheeks with nervous fingers. She wasn't beautiful, not like Sophie anyway, who seemed set to rival their mother's looks when she'd been young. Paige had expressive green eyes and a generous mouth, but her features were not particularly memorable, which was why she'd never really believed that any of the men she'd dated had wanted her for herself.

A knock at the door aroused her apprehension. What

now? she wondered anxiously, but it was only Sophie, who came into the room without waiting for a response. She'd changed, too, but the yellow slip dress she was wearing barely covered her bottom, and her clunky wedges clomped across the rug.

'Are you ready?' she asked, viewing Paige's appearance with critical eyes. 'Is that new? I don't remember seeing it before.'

'It's not new,' said Paige, wondering if she dared broach the subject of Sophie's appearance, but her sister just pulled a face and sauntered over to the balcony doors.

'I wonder what the view's like from here?' she mused, drawing back as a particularly large moth came and fluttered against the glass. 'You did say you'd stayed here before, didn't you? I couldn't see much of the island as we drove up from the harbour, but the house seemed huge.'

'It is.' Paige chose her words with care. 'Is that what you're wearing for dinner?'

'Well, I'm not going to get changed again,' retorted Sophie, swinging round. She looked down at her dress. 'What's wrong with it?'

Paige hesitated. 'Nothing, I suppose—'

'Just because you like to wear frumpy clothes doesn't mean I have to.' Sophie's jaw jutted belligerently. 'I bet Paris would approve.'

Paige shrugged. 'I dare say he would, if he could see you,' she declared evenly. 'But until we know what our position is here—'

'I thought we did know,' countered Sophie, frowning. 'We're going to keep some old man's ward company. But don't expect me to dress like a nanny. You can, but I've got better things to do.'

Paige shook her head, deciding not to pursue it right now, and changed the subject. 'So,' she said pleasantly, 'have you unpacked your things and put them away?'

'I've unpacked some,' said Sophie carelessly. 'I'll do the

rest in the morning.' She scowled suddenly, turning on her high heels that added inches to her five-feet-six-inch height. 'Hey, your room is bigger than mine. That's not fair.'

Paige glanced about her. In all honesty, she'd paid little attention to the spacious apartment she'd been given. She'd noticed the bed was square, with a solid wooden frame, and that the quilt that covered it was made of hand-woven silk. But she'd scarcely admired the carved oak furniture or heeded the high arching ceiling above her head. There were rose chiffon curtains at the windows, she saw now, and richly patterned rugs dotted about the polished floor. In other circumstances, she wouldn't have failed to be charmed by its simple elegance, and she could understand why Sophie was so impressed.

'Do you want to swap?' she asked.

'No.' Sophie had the grace to look slightly shamefaced now. 'I was just admiring it, that's all.' She went to take a look into the adjoining bathroom. 'I think my bathroom's bigger than yours.'

'Good.'

Paige decided it was time they were leaving. It was no use putting it off any longer, however apprehensive she felt. She took another look at herself in the mirror, and tucked a loose strand of brown-gold hair behind her ear. Then, after checking that the gold hoops she was wearing in her ears were secure, she picked up her purse and turned towards the door.

'Shall we—?'

'This guy—'

They both spoke together, and although Paige wasn't sure she wanted to hear what her sister had been going to say she knew they couldn't leave until she did.

'Nikolas Petronides,' went on Sophie, after receiving a silent go-ahead, 'he must be filthy rich, mustn't he? I mean, according to Paris, he owns a fleet of oil tankers and you have to admit, this house is something else.'

Paige suppressed a groan. The last thing she needed was for Sophie to start getting ideas about Nikolas. And she hadn't even seen him yet! Her sister thought he was old, but Nikolas was only about forty. And he was still a disturbingly attractive man.

'I don't think that's of any interest to us,' she declared reprovingly, as if talking about Nikolas didn't bother her in the least. Didn't remind her of the first time she been introduced to him by her father, or of the hot dark eyes that had seduced her on the spot...

'Get real, Paige. I wouldn't mind marrying someone with pots of money,' retorted Sophie, with a grimace. 'I wonder how he'd feel about taking a child-bride?' She giggled, and Paige knew an almost irresistible impulse to slap her. 'Or perhaps he has a son. What do you think?'

'I think you're being very silly,' said Paige, aware that she was overreacting. But right now she couldn't think about Nikolas without remembering the past they'd shared. It was this house, she thought. It had so many connotations—even though he'd never made love to her here...

'What's silly about wanting to marry a millionaire?' exclaimed Sophie at once. 'Or wanting to know if he has a son?'

'He doesn't.'

Paige was abrupt, and Sophie's eyes widened. 'Of course,' she blurted excitedly. 'You've met him. I'd forgotten about that. Go on: tell me what he's like.'

'Not now.' Paige was determined not to get into that discussion. 'Come on, we're going to be late for dinner.'

'So what? Petronides isn't here. You heard what that old witch said when we arrived. I'm not worried about keeping some Greek schoolkid waiting.'

Paige forbore to mention that the Greek schoolkid in question was a year older than she was. And, looking at Sophie as they left the bedroom and started along the upper gallery, she was reluctantly aware that the younger girl was probably years older when it came to experience of life. Ariadne might have lost both her parents, but she hadn't been left alone. She'd been protected and cared for all the time she was grieving, and she had the comfort of knowing that her future was secure.

But now was not the time to be having negative thoughts about the girl she'd come here to chaperon. Instead, Paige concentrated on her surroundings, finding that her memory hadn't deserted her when they reached the top of the stairs. Marble treads led down to an Italian marble foyer, a black iron balustrade following their sweeping curve.

'Wow!' Sophie was impressed, and she paused on the first stair to admire the cut-glass chandelier that illuminated the hall below. 'What a pity we don't have an audience,' she taunted. 'We could make quite an entrance from here.'

'Thank goodness we don't—' Paige was beginning, when a tall figure moved out of the shadows and into the light.

'*Parakalo,*' said Nikolas, a black silk shirt and black trousers accentuating his darkly tanned appearance. 'Please—Sophie, is it not?—feel free to descend the stairs any way you choose.'

Even Sophie was taken aback and Paige wished she could just fade into the woodwork behind her. Evidently Nikolas had returned and it was him they'd been keeping waiting. Always supposing he intended to eat with the hired help this evening, of course. Until she knew what their position in the household was going to be, she couldn't be sure of anything.

'Is that *him*?'

Sophie's stage whisper must have reached Nikolas and Paige gave her sister an exasperated look. 'Go on,' she urged, pushing the girl forward without answering her, and Sophie returned her look with interest before obediently starting down.

'I only asked,' she muttered, but Paige wasn't in the

mood to be placated. She was already wondering how she'd ever thought that bringing Sophie here would be a good idea.

Nikolas had stepped back as they came down the stairs but now he approached them, greeting them in his own language as if to reassure them that he hadn't heard what Sophie had said. '*Kalispera,*' he said, his deep voice scraping across Paige's already frayed nerves. '*Kalos orissate sto Skiapolis.*'

Sophie blinked, clearly not understanding his words, and he took her hand and said easily, 'Welcome to Skiapolis. Did you have a good journey?'

'Oh—yes. Thank you.' Paige was amazed to see that her sister had actually turned fiery red. 'I'm sorry about—you know—saying what I did. But this house is, like—way cool.'

'I am glad you like it,' he responded smoothly, but Paige closed her eyes for a moment, praying for deliverance. She dreaded to think what Sophie was going to say next and she started violently when Nikolas murmured, 'Paige?' in a concerned voice. 'Are you all right?'

He was standing in front of her now and she had no choice but to allow him to shake her hand, too. But her fingers tingled within the strong grasp of his, her damp palm sliding revealingly against his firm flesh.

'I—I'm fine,' she managed, extracting her hand again as soon as she possibly could. He was so close, much closer than he'd been across the table at the restaurant in London, and she was instantly conscious of his height and the broadness of his shoulders, and the intimidating awareness that this might not have been such a good idea on her part either. 'I'm sorry if we've kept you waiting. Your housekeeper said you were away.'

'I was. But now I'm back.' Nikolas continued to regard her with considering eyes, and Paige, whose eyes were on a level with the opened collar of his shirt, concentrated on

the V of dark hair that was visible above the placket.
'You're flushed, *aghapita*. Are you not feeling well?'

'I've told you, I'm fine—' Paige started protestingly,
only to be overridden by her sister's voice.

'She didn't eat any lunch on the plane,' Sophie told him
smugly, not to be outdone, and as if realising they had an
audience Nikolas took an automatic step away.

'That was unwise,' he said softly, his eyes lingering on
her embarrassed face. 'Was it so stressful? The journey, I
mean.'

'No. No, of course not.'

Paige wished he would leave her alone. Sophie wasn't a
fool and if he continued to behave as if her well-being was
of some importance to him her sister would begin to suspect she had something to hide.

But perhaps that was his intention, she mused uneasily.
She'd never truly believed he'd offered her this job out of
the goodness of his heart. Men like Nikolas Petronides
didn't forgive—or forget. And, although she had no illusions that she'd ever meant a great deal to him, she had
walked out on him, which in his eyes was probably unforgivable.

'*Kala*,' he murmured now, inclining his head towards a
room on his left. 'Ariadne is waiting for us. We will go
and introduce you, *ne*?'

Paige nodded, glancing at Sophie before accompanying
him across the vast expanse of marble that lay between
them and what she seemed to recall from her previous visit
was an elegant drawing room. Around them, the plain walls
of the reception hall were hung with literally dozens of
paintings, large and small, that added vivid colour to what
was essentially a neutral area. But there were flowers, too:
huge bouquets of magnolia and oleander and lily in
sculpted vases, whose distinctive fragrance hung sweetly in
the cool conditioned air. It was all very beautiful and very

civilised, and Paige wished she could relax and stop thinking that she'd made a terrible mistake.

The lamplit salon they entered was as she remembered: high ceilings above striped silk walls; long undraped windows at either side of an enormous stone fireplace, above which hung an impressive portrait of a woman she knew to be Nikolas's mother; several upholstered sofas in green and gold; and rich, subtly woven rugs scattered over a polished floor. The many display cabinets were the repository for delicate china and ceramics, a collection Nikolas's grandfather had begun in his lifetime and which his late father had continued. And, although there were other paintings here, too, there were also a handful of jewelled icons to draw the eye. It was a beautiful room, casually luxurious, yet revealing a lived-in comfort and informality in the sprinkling of cushions on the sofas, in the sprawl of magazines decorating a low granite table, and the squat vase of wild flowers residing on the mantel.

But it was the girl who was standing on the hearth who took Paige's eye. Ariadne—Stephanopoulous, as Donald Jamieson had advised her—was nothing like the schoolgirl she had been expecting. Tall and slender, with a long coil of night-dark hair hanging over her shoulder, she looked years older than the seventeen she admitted to. She was wearing black: an ankle-length gown that moulded her figure, and would not have looked out of place on a woman twice her age. She looked more like Nikolas's wife than his ward, thought Paige in some dismay, wondering how on earth she was supposed to deal with her.

And, indeed, Ariadne reacted to their appearance with the kind of studied arrogance that seemed to confirm Paige's assessment of her. 'Nikolas!' she exclaimed, ignoring the two women with him and going towards him, her hands held out in front of her so that he was obliged to take them in his own. *'Ola entaksi?'*

'Speak English, Ariadne,' Nikolas chided her mildly.

'Our guests are not familiar with our language. And, after all, that is one of the reasons I have invited Miss Tennant here: to help you improve your accent.'

'My accent doesn't need improving,' retorted Ariadne at once, with a little less maturity. But Paige had to admit she was right. The Greek girl appeared to speak English very well indeed. A lot better than the schoolgirl Greek she could manage.

'Whatever...' Nikolas's tone had hardened now. He turned to Paige. 'My ward,' he said simply. 'I hope you'll become good friends.'

'I hope so, too,' said Paige firmly, taking the limp hand Ariadne offered her. 'It's very nice to meet you, Miss Stephanopoulous.'

'Miss Stephanopoulous!' Nikolas was impatient. 'Her name is Ariadne.' He glanced at the girl beside her. 'And this is Sophie. Miss Tennant's sister.'

'Hi.' Sophie greeted the other girl without enthusiasm, and Paige hoped she wouldn't say anything too outrageous. 'I guess we're the same age, right?'

'Are we?' Ariadne sounded bored, and she immediately turned back to her guardian, wrapping her hands around his forearm and gazing up at him with wide, appealing eyes. '*Isos*—maybe we can have dinner now?'

'After I have offered Miss Tennant and her sister an aperitif,' Nikolas answered evenly, removing her hands from his wrist. 'Paige?' He indicated that she should follow him across to an ebony drinks cabinet. 'What will you have?'

Paige hesitated; then, after exchanging a warning look with Sophie, she crossed the room. She wasn't happy about leaving the two girls alone, and she kept glancing back over her shoulder as if she expected something awful to happen.

'Ouzo? Retsina? Or something more familiar?' asked Nikolas at her approach. 'And relax. It will do Ariadne good to spend time with someone of her own age for a change.'

Paige expelled a breath. 'I thought you said she still attended school.'

'I did.' Nikolas lifted a bottle of white wine from the refrigerated cabinet and arched an enquiring brow. Then, after she'd nodded her approval, he went on, 'But Ariadne has been too much with older people this past year. She's had a series of minor infections which have kept her away from school, and I had to hire a tutor to give her extra lessons.'

'I see.' Paige watched him pour her wine. 'She seems very—attached to you.'

'You noticed.'

'It would have been hard not to.' Paige took the glass he offered, carefully avoiding his fingers, and then looked up to find him watching her with a whimsical expression. 'What?' she exclaimed. Then, glancing over her shoulder again, she said, 'Well—she's hardly discreet.'

'Unlike you,' he remarked drily, pouring a generous measure of Scotch into a cut-glass tumbler. 'I must admit I was surprised when I heard that you'd been in touch with Jamieson. If I'd thought for a minute that you'd change your mind, I'd have hung on for a few more days. Why did you?'

'Why did I what?'

He pulled a wry face. 'Don't pretend you don't know what I'm talking about.'

'Oh—' Paige knew she should have been prepared for the question, but she wasn't. 'I—I decided it was too good an opportunity to miss.'

'Did you?'

His eyes were lazily intent and she hurried to explain herself. 'Financially, I mean,' she assured him. 'And although it meant taking Sophie out of school a couple of weeks early all her exams are over.'

'Ah, yes, Sophie.' His eyes moved past her to where her

sister was waiting, a look of resentment on her face now. 'She's not at all like you, is she?'

Paige shrugged. 'If you say so.'

'I do.' His mouth took on a sensual curve. 'And before I ask your sister what she would like to drink, let me say that you have many advantages that she has not.'

'I'm older, you mean?'

Paige refused to let him disconcert her, and Nikolas's eyes narrowed on her tense face. 'Older, of course. But age has its compensations. You know what I am saying,' he added softly, and then broke off as an argument erupted across the room.

'Who the f—? I mean, who the hell do you think you are?' Sophie's voice rose in outrage. 'You can't speak to me like that. You're not the mistress here!'

'*Arketa! Arketa!* That is enough!'

As Ariadne opened her mouth to respond, Nikolas slammed down his drink and strode across the room. For a moment, he seemed to have forgotten his command that they should speak English, and his initial remonstrance was issued in the language of his youth.

Then, as if realising that Sophie couldn't understand him, he gathered himself, and when he spoke again his manner was more controlled. 'Ariadne,' he snapped. 'Do you want to tell me what is going on? What have you been saying to upset our guest?'

Ariadne looked indignant at first. And then, as if realising her guardian was not going to respond to that kind of attitude, she mumbled, 'It was nothing, Nikolas. Really. I was merely saying that Kiria Papandreiu docs not likc to kccp dinner waiting.'

'That's not true.' Sophie didn't mince her words. 'What she actually said was that we weren't welcome here; that she saw no reason why she had to put herself out for people she didn't even like.'

Paige, who was behind Nikolas now, had the feeling that

her sister had edited the exchange for their benefit. Or perhaps she hadn't understood everything the Greek girl had said. Whatever, judging from Ariadne's smug expression, she had said something to cause offence, and there was an awkward silence as Nikolas assessed the situation.

'Is this true, Ariadne?' he asked at last, and the smugness disappeared to be replaced with wounded indignation.

'Of course not!' she exclaimed, ignoring Sophie's cry of protest. 'I'm afraid she misunderstood what I was saying.'

Nikolas breathed deeply. 'Is that so?' he said heavily, and Sophie immediately jumped to her own defence.

'No, it's not,' she argued hotly. 'I wouldn't make up something like that. Tell him, Paige. I'm not a liar. She's just a jealous cow who seems to think that wearing granny clothes gives her the right to—'

'Shut up, Sophie.'

Paige broke in now, aware that she didn't really know who to believe. Until recently, she'd have believed Sophie without hesitation, but after the incident with the heroin she couldn't be sure.

'Oh, right.' Her sister was glaring mutinously at her now, and Paige realised she'd switched the blame. 'Thanks a bunch. She bad-mouths both of us and I'm the one who gets dumped on.'

'Nobody is being—what was the expression you used?— dumped on,' declared Nikolas bleakly. 'As far as I am concerned, the matter is closed. Whatever was said—' he looked at each of them in turn '—you *will* get on with one another. Whatever happens, I do not intend to make any other arrangement. That is my decision. *Katalavenete?*'

Paige was fully prepared for Sophie to turn on him as she'd turned on her more times than she cared to remember in the past six months. But she didn't. With a careless shrug of her shoulders, she appeared to accept what he'd said, and it was left to Ariadne to express her resentment.

'But I said nothing, Nikolas,' his ward murmured plaintively, her look of pained distress not fooling Paige for a minute. She had the uneasy feeling that Sophie had been telling the truth all along, while she had no real idea what was going on behind Ariadne's innocent mask.

'As I told you, we will say no more about it,' said her guardian flatly. 'And now I suggest you offer Sophie a soda before we go into dinner.'

# CHAPTER FOUR

PAIGE did not sleep well.

She should have done so. After all, she was very tired, her bed was superbly comfortable, and there were none of the outside disturbances that had disrupted her nights at the bed-and-breakfast.

But it didn't work out that way. She tossed and turned for hours, continually replaying the events of the evening in her mind until she was hot and sweaty and too over-wrought to relax. Her brain buzzed with the realisation that this was not going to be the escape from Sophie's problems she'd consoled herself it would be. Ariadne was not the placid schoolgirl she'd imagined; she didn't want them here, and her relationship with Nikolas was not the simple one Paige had expected. Sophie had been right; Ariadne was jealous—probably of anyone who distracted her guardian's attention from herself—and Paige suspected she was going to do everything in her power to make their stay on Skiapolis as unpleasant as possible.

Which didn't make for an easy night. Paige eventually fell into a shallow slumber towards dawn, but she was up again as soon as it was light, taking a shower, tidying her room, writing a few lines to Aunt Ingrid at the bureau in her bedroom. It wasn't easy finding the right words to describe their arrival to her aunt either, and she contented herself by sticking to the facts and not attempting to touch on any more personal matters.

It was still only seven o'clock when she stepped out onto her balcony and took her first real look at the view from her window. It was as spectacular as she'd expected, a sweeping panorama that encompassed the tiny port of

Agios Petros on the western side of the island, and the wooded slopes below the villa that fell away to a private beach. Paige knew that below the cliffs that hid the shoreline there was a wooden jetty where she and her father had landed from Nikolas's yacht four years ago. A dinghy had ferried them the short distance from the yacht itself, which had been anchored out in the bay, and she remembered gazing up at the villa as they sped across the water and thinking she had never seen a more beautiful house in her life

But such memories were not welcome now, and Paige turned her gaze to the small town. Flat-roofed, white-washed dwellings clustered around the harbour, their steep, cobble-stoned streets something she did remember with affection from the evening before. She could see the tall cupola of a church and the sails of a windmill, turning in the warm breeze that blew off the ocean, and the simple beauty of it all was impossible to deny. She determined there and then that, whatever happened, she was not going to let anyone intimidate her. Neither Ariadne nor Nikolas. She was here to do a job and she was going to do it, however difficult it might prove to be.

Turning back into the bedroom, she decided she might as well act upon it right away. If she stayed up here any longer, she was likely to lose what little confidence she'd found, and after running a brush through her hair she opened her door and went out onto the gallery.

She'd hesitated over what she should wear for her first morning as Ariadne's companion and had finally decided to choose the kind of outfit she'd have worn if she'd been a regular visitor to the island. A butter-yellow T-shirt and matching shorts might not meet with Ariadne's approval but she'd determined to start as she meant to go on. If Nikolas did not approve of such leniency in her dress, he would have to tell her. Until then, she intended to please herself.

Her feet, in white canvas deck shoes, made little sound on the polished floor and she reached the head of the stairs without incident. She felt a bit mean passing Sophie's door without telling her where she was going, but her sister was unlikely to be awake yet and she was looking forward to having a few minutes on her own.

One of the maids who had been on duty in the dining room the night before was dusting the elegant pillars that supported the balustrade. She gave Paige a polite smile as she passed, but apart from a mumbled, *'Kalimera, kiria,'* she didn't attempt to detain her. Paige returned the greeting, the Greek words rolling instinctively off her tongue. Perhaps she should try to improve her knowledge of the language while she was here, she thought consideringly. It was possible it might be of some value in the future.

She couldn't help wondering what the maid had thought of the dinner party she'd served in the family dining room the night before. Nikolas had described the room as intimate, and she supposed it was compared to the formal rooms she'd seen before. Easily thirty feet square, with an oblong maple table and six matching chairs upholstered in gold silk brocade, it was hardly homey, but it did give some indication of the size of the rest of the house.

Still, it wasn't the room Paige was thinking about right now. She was remembering the meal, and the uncomfortable silence that had reigned after Nikolas had been called away. Until then, he'd done his best to entertain them, delighting Sophie with anecdotes about the famous people who'd stayed on Skiapolis, and she'd been disappointed when one of the menservants had come to tell him he had an urgent call.

Paige had wondered, rather uncharitably, she was sure, if Nikolas had arranged it that way; if he'd left the three women alone together in the hope that they'd settle their differences. If so, he couldn't have been more wrong. Despite all her efforts, Ariadne had given monosyllabic answers to everything Paige had said. She only came to life when she was giving the servants orders—just as if she considered herself the mistress of the house, Paige reflected. Exactly as Sophie had said.

It hadn't been easy for Paige, being treated as if she were no older than her sister, as if her opinion were of no consequence. But it had been their first day, she'd been tired, and she hadn't had the energy to assert herself. Besides, she hadn't wanted to get into an argument with Ariadne, not over anything so trivial.

The huge reception hall was empty, she saw now, glancing about her. She smiled, enchanted anew by the beauty of her surroundings, by the paintings, and the flowers, and the exquisite pieces of sculpture that she saw now were half hidden in niches in the walls. The scent of the beeswax the maid had been using mingled with the perfumes of the flowers, drawing her towards the open doorway where they'd entered the night before.

Outside, a cool verandah stretched in either direction, while ahead of her shallow steps led down to the formal gardens that surrounded the villa. The sun was gaining strength and as she walked to the top of the steps its heat was warm on her bare arms. It was a perfect morning, the sky a bowl of china blue overhead. Despite her thoughts, she found her spirits lifting. Surely in a place like this nothing could be all that bad?

The sun-baked walls of the villa curved away for quite a distance, blending into other buildings that she guessed housed some of the servants she'd met the night before. There would obviously be garages, too, and perhaps some stables. She knew Nikolas enjoyed riding. She'd ridden with him when she was here before.

When she was here before...

Resting her hands on the pillared walls that edged the verandah, she felt the warmth of the sun beneath her fingers. She took a deep breath, trying to regain her earlier optimism, and then started in surprise when a low, amused voice remarked, 'How did I know you would be up?'

She'd been so absorbed in her thoughts, so intent on the unhappy memories of the past, that she hadn't heard his approach. He was standing in the doorway behind her, his shoulder propped idly against the pillar. In a black T-shirt and loose white cotton trousers, his dark hair tumbling over his forehead, he looked big and broad, and undeniably sexy, and years younger than she knew him to be. But then, she had never thought of Nikolas as being that much older than herself.

'Nikolas,' she acknowledged him now, straightening, not knowing what to do with her hands for a moment and then stuffing them into the pockets of her shorts. 'I— Good morning.'

'Good morning.' He left the doorway to come towards her. 'Did you sleep well?' he asked, and then shocked her into immobility when he brushed his fingers across the hollows beneath her eyes. 'Ah, no.' He answered his own question. 'I see you did not. Poor Paige. Coming here has been stressful for you, has it not?'

'What did you expect?'

Paige was stung into an involuntary response by the sensuous touch of his knuckles against her cheeks. He was playing with her, she thought unsteadily. He was enjoying having her at a disadvantage.

'What did I expect?' he echoed now as she flinched away from his hand. 'I don't know. That you might have realised I was trying to help you? That we might be able to forget the past?'

'As I've told you before, don't patronise me, Nikolas.'

His brows arched. '*Me sinhorite.* I'm sorry,' he corrected himself quickly. 'I didn't realise. Obviously, I shall have to be careful what I say in future.'

'That's not necessary.' Paige sighed impatiently. 'I'm

here, aren't I? I wouldn't have accepted the job if I hadn't thought that we—that *I*—could make it work.'

'No.'

But Nikolas's expression was unreadable, and when he came to rest his broad, long-fingered hands on the wall beside her she knew a sudden urge to get away from him. She didn't want them to become familiar with one another again; she didn't want to feel this unwelcome softening towards him. She wanted to remember he'd been using her just as much as he thought she'd been using him, and his only regret had been that she had ended their affair before he'd had the chance to do so.

'I—I think I'll go for a walk,' she said now, moving towards the steps that led down to the gardens. It was getting hot and she had no protection for her skin, but she didn't intend to stay out long.

'If you'll permit me, I'll join you,' he said at once, and she realised there was no escape.

But she had to try. 'Oh, please,' she murmured. 'I'm sure you have better things to do.' Her eyes challenged his. 'And your ward might wonder where you are.'

'She might,' he conceded carelessly. He followed her down the steps, his trousers billowing against his muscled thighs. 'But it will give us an opportunity to discuss your— what shall we call them?—your duties, *ne*? As you pointed out so charmingly, you are here to do a job of work.'

Paige shrugged as he joined her on the paved path below the verandah. 'If you say so, Nikolas,' she replied tightly. 'Or would you rather I called you Kirie Petronides instead?'

'Nikolas will do,' he answered shortly, his nostrils flaring with sudden impatience. He gestured for her to precede him. 'We will go this way.'

Paige decided not to argue in the circumstances. She accompanied him along a vine-shaded pathway that led along the side of the house. A pergola-like arch, overhung with roses, brought them around a corner and onto a sprawling terrace, where the shell of a swimming pool glistened in the sun. Beyond the terrace, the lush greenery sloped away towards the rocky grandeur of the cliffs.

They walked that way, down through orchards of peach and citrus trees, buzzing with insects and heady with the scent of the fruit. Underfoot, dwarf orchids and other plants grew in wild profusion, the grass still cool from the dampness of the dew.

But it was hot. Paige could feel herself sweating, beads of perspiration causing honey-gold strands of hair to cling to the back of her neck. Her forehead, too, was drenched with moisture, and she surreptitiously wiped her wrist across it as they walked.

She was thirsty, which was probably responsible for the slight ache that was developing in her temples. She wasn't used to such intense heat so early in the day. The only relief to be had was by walking in Nikolas's shadow, but that wasn't always easy when she didn't want him to notice what she was doing.

They stopped at the top of the steps that led down to the private beach. There was a seat there, etched into the limestone of the cliffs, that provided a small oasis of shade. Trying not to look too eager, Paige moved gratefully into the overhang, raising her arms without thinking to lift the hair from her neck.

'You're tired,' said Nikolas, putting one foot on the bench beside her, and she was immediately conscious of how provocative her action had been. Lifting her arms had caused her breasts to press against the thin fabric of her T-shirt, and although she was sure her bra was adequate she could feel their arousal for herself.

But it was difficult to read his expression. With eyes dazzled from the sun, all that was evident was the concern in his voice. 'Just—hot,' she contradicted him, not wanting him to think she might not be capable of doing the job he'd hired her for. She licked her dry lips and concentrated on the ocean. 'Um—I thought your yacht would be anchored out in the bay.'

Nikolas dropped his foot and turned to look where she was looking. 'Why would you think that?' he asked. 'I keep it in Piraeus, as you know.'

'I just thought—' Paige gave an awkward shrug. 'I wondered about your arrival.'

'Ah.' He nodded. 'You didn't hear the helicopter, then?'

'No.'

Paige shook her head, but with hindsight she did recall hearing a noise the evening before. It had been while she was taking her shower and she'd assumed it was just a low-flying aircraft. It was obvious now that it had been a helicopter instead.

'It is a much more efficient means of getting here from the mainland,' he told her. 'And, before you ask, I did not know if I would be able to get away last night, or naturally I would have arranged for you and Sophie to join me.'

Paige sank down onto the bench. 'I wasn't implying—'

'Did I say you were?' Her eyes had adjusted now and she could see the faint flare of irritation he was controlling. 'So—' He came down on the bench beside her. 'Tell me why you really changed your mind.'

Paige took a deep breath, and then wished she hadn't. She was far too conscious of him as it was, and smelling the distinctive scent of his cologne mixing with the slightly musky odour of his body was disturbing to say the least. All she could think about was his nearness, and the urge she had to touch his flesh.

'I told you,' she said, tension bringing a betraying sharpness to her tone, and he regarded her with dark, disbelieving eyes.

'You also told me you wouldn't work for me,' he reminded her softly. 'You knew your circumstances were desperate before you left the restaurant, yet you were painfully insistent that you were not—how did you put it? Oh, yes. You were not *for sale.*'

Paige blew out a breath. Dear God, what could she tell him? If he refused to accept her explanation, such as it was, what could she say? If she told him they'd left England because she'd found out that Sophie was getting involved with the drug scene, what would he think of her then? He might even decide that it was too high a price to pay for his revenge.

'Does it matter?' she muttered now, the headache that had plagued her ever since they'd left the villa becoming more insistent. She'd been foolish to allow her pride to overrule her head. But she'd been afraid that if she'd said she was going to have breakfast he'd have joined her. As it had turned out, she hadn't gained any advantage.

'I think so,' he declared now, turning to look at her, and although her face was turned away something in her manner must have betrayed her weakness. 'You are not well,' he added, cool fingers on her nape discovering her racing pulse. 'The sun is an unforgiving enemy. I will take you back to the villa.'

'There's no need—'

'There's every need,' he interrupted her harshly, and his fingers on her neck tightened for a moment to turn her face to his. 'We will continue this conversation at some other time,' he told her, allowing his hand to slide away across her shoulder and down her arm. She shivered then, and his mouth curved with sudden irony. 'Do not lie to me, *aghapita*. We know one another far too well for that.'

It seemed an incredibly long walk back to the house, but Nikolas kept a restraining hand on her arm, not allowing her to go too fast. Perhaps he'd guessed that, left to herself, she'd have raced back; that, despite her throbbing head, she just wanted to get away from him.

As it was, she couldn't ignore the possession in the strong fingers that detained her, or deny the dark power that both attracted and repelled in equal measures. She mustn't allow him to know he had any kind of control over her emotions, she told herself, and then expelled a sigh of resignation when they emerged from the trees to find Ariadne breakfasting on the terrace.

It was an enviable spot. The round white-clothed table was protected by a striped umbrella. It was set outside open French doors, one level up from the curving swimming pool, the reflection of the water dancing on the swaying canopy.

Ariadne was wearing white this morning: a loose, long-sleeved white tunic over white leggings that hugged her slender form. She evidently didn't feel the heat or, if she did, she managed not to show it. Whereas Paige, in only shorts and a T-shirt, couldn't wait to strip them off.

Nikolas's hand fell away from her arm as they stepped up onto the terrace, though he kept pace with her as they crossed the patio. Still, his attention was diverted as Ariadne rose to her feet and came to meet them, and Paige wondered if she could escape into the house without any-one noticing.

'*Kalimera*, Nikolas,' Ariadne greeted her guardian warmly, reaching up to bestow an eager kiss on his lean, tanned cheek. Then, because she had learned her lesson, she added, 'Good morning, Miss Tennant. You look very hot. I do not think our climate agrees with you.'

Paige gave her a thin smile, giving up any hope of mak-ing a hasty exit. 'I'll get used to it,' she said, not prepared to be patronised again.

'It's my fault,' put in Nikolas gallantly. 'I invited Miss Tennant to join me in a walk.' His eyes narrowed as he turned back to Paige, as if daring her to contradict him. 'Do you have some cream to put on your arms and legs? I fear the sun has already staked a claim.'

'I'll be fine,' Paige assured him, but before she could

excuse herself his hand in the small of her back urged her towards the table.

'Come,' he said. 'We will join Ariadne. I will ask Kiria Papandreiu if she has some aspirin for your headache.'

'Oh, really, I—'

Paige wanted to refuse, but Nikolas had already approached the table, picking up a glass and filling it from the jug of freshly squeezed orange juice beside Ariadne's plate. 'There,' he said as she hesitated, and Paige subsided onto one of the wrought-iron chairs. 'Drink this,' he added, handing the glass to her. 'It will make you feel better. It's full of Vitamin C.'

Paige doubted if anything could make her feel better, short of lying down in a darkened room, but in fact the orange juice did help. Even with Ariadne glaring at her from across the table when Nikolas wasn't looking, she found the drink cool and refreshing, so much so that she could view the basket of sweet rolls and honeyed pastries without revulsion.

Kiria Papandreiu appeared to serve them herself. After ordering fresh coffee for himself and his guest, Paige heard Nikolas ask if she had any *aspirini* for Kiria Tennant. The housekeeper answered in the affirmative, and Paige resigned herself to staying where she was. Besides, there was a breeze here that had not been evident out in the open, and its coolness was helping her to relax.

'Miss Tennant has a headache, too?' Ariadne only just managed to keep the satisfaction out of her voice. 'Oughtn't she to go and lie down?'

'It's just a slight headache,' Paige found herself replying, and then raised defensive eyes to Nikolas's face. 'It is,' she insisted. 'I'm feeling much better already.' She deliberately leaned back in her chair. 'The heat has never bothered me before.'

Ariadne looked sceptical. 'You're used to the heat, Miss Tennant?' Her mockery was evident. 'You're used to spending your—what is it?—two weeks' holiday in the sun?'

'Actually, we used to spend several months in the South of France in summer,' Paige corrected her, biting back the urge to tell her about Nikolas. She could imagine the girl's chagrin if she reminisced about their relationship or mentioned that she and her father had spent a few days on Nikolas's yacht.

But that was petty, and she had no desire to start a feud with the girl. Or continue one, she added wryly, aware that Ariadne was already looking for trouble. In any case, it seemed fairly obvious that Nikolas hadn't told his ward that they'd known one another before she'd taken up this appointment, and it wasn't up to her to bring it up.

But Ariadne wouldn't leave it alone. She waited impatiently while the housekeeper served them with fresh coffee, fresh orange juice, and another basket of warm pastries, and then returned to the subject again.

Watching Paige take two of the aspirin from the bottle Kiria Papandreiu had brought for her, she asked, 'What did you do in the South of France, Miss Tennant? Were you working at one of the hotels?'

Paige almost choked on one of the tablets, but somehow she managed to get it down. 'No,' she said, beating Nikolas to it. 'I wasn't working at that time. I was still at school.'

'So this is a long time ago,' suggested Ariadne innocently, and Nikolas fixed her with a warning look.

'It's not your concern,' he said. 'Miss Tennant's private life is her own. And what she did before she came here is of no importance to you.'

'Oh, but Nikolas...' Ariadne adopted the wounded air she'd assumed the evening before. 'I was interested, that is all, *aghapitos*. If we are to be friends, there should be no secrets between us.'

'Friends do not ask personal questions,' retorted her guardian, reaching for the coffee pot and pouring some into

Paige's cup. 'Come...' He picked up the basket of rolls and offered it to her. 'We have still not discussed what your duties here are going to be.'

'I do not need a nursemaid, Nikolas,' put in Ariadne sulkily before Paige could answer him, and she heard his indrawn breath as he controlled his temper.

'No,' he conceded, with the utmost patience, 'but you do need a companion. Someone who can keep you company when I return to Athens.'

'But I want to return to Athens, too,' protested Ariadne, and Paige guessed that this was the crux of the problem. Nikolas was responsible for the girl but he was finding it difficult to look after her and maintain the workload he'd inherited from his father when he retired. It was a relief to feel that she was needed; that the job he'd offered her was genuine, after all.

'It is—better for your health if you stay here on the island,' said Nikolas now, helping himself to coffee. Paige noticed he didn't eat anything, but she guessed he'd had breakfast earlier. 'You've become far too susceptible to infection, Ariadne. You know that. Staying here will give you time to regain your strength; to relax.'

Ariadne was not to be placated. 'What you mean is, you do not want me with you,' she accused him, and Nikolas breathed through his nose as he endeavoured to be polite.

'What I want is not part of this equation,' he told her. He sighed. 'Athens is not the place to be in the height of summer. It is hot, and much too busy. In any case, you are safer here.'

'But I want to be with you—'

'That is not possible, Ariadne.'

Nikolas swallowed half his coffee in one gulp, but when he would have turned to Paige the girl spoke again. 'Why not?' she pleaded. 'I will not be a nuisance to you. And you know I am only ill when you are not around.'

'*Ftani pya!*'

In his urgency to bring the discussion to an end, Nikolas resorted to his own language, and Paige realised it was a measure of his frustration that he didn't even notice.

But Ariadne did. 'Why are you speaking Greek, Nikolas?' she demanded. 'Do you not wish Miss Tennant to know that we have become such—close friends?'

'I warn you, Ariadne—'

Paige got abruptly to her feet. She had no wish to witness any more of this humiliating display. It was embarrassing listening to Ariadne demean herself, and although she had little sympathy for the girl she couldn't help the suspicion that Nikolas had brought this upon himself. He had obviously allowed Ariadne to have her own way for far too long, and now he was paying the price.

'If you don't mind, I'd like to go and take a shower,' she murmured as she pushed back from the table. 'Perhaps we could discuss what you want me to do at some other time.'

Nikolas rose to face her. 'But you've hardly eaten anything.'

'I'd really rather get a shower,' Paige insisted, not wanting another altercation. 'If you'll excuse me…'

He let her go without further argument and Paige hurried across the patio towards the house. Only to come face to face with Sophie who was just coming out.

'Hey, Paige.'

Her sister sounded cheerful for once and Paige refused to show the dismay she felt when she saw what Sophie was wearing. In a pink spandex top and frayed denim shorts, her sister was obviously making a statement. But Paige was too eager to get away to care about that now.

'I'll see you later,' she said, letting Sophie make what she liked of that, but she couldn't prevent a smile from tugging at her lips at the thought of Nikolas's reaction as she went into the house.

# CHAPTER FIVE

WHEN Paige emerged from the bathroom some twenty minutes later, she found that someone had left a tray containing coffee, rolls and fresh fruit on the table in her bedroom. She didn't want to believe it was Nikolas who had been so thoughtful, but who else could it be? And she was grateful. Now that she was clean and cool again, she was starving, and she crunched on a crisp apple as she dried her hair.

Then, after eating one of the rolls and drinking a cup of coffee, she dressed in a simple linen shift that exposed her knees. She refused to cover herself up, as Ariadne had done, but she wanted no comparisons to be drawn between her and Sophie either.

Besides, the apricot linen was flattering to her pale cream colouring. And, with her hair newly washed, and curling against her nape, she looked decidedly less harassed than she'd done earlier. A touch of brown eye-shadow and a bronze gloss for her lips completed her toilette, and, content that she could hold her own with a schoolgirl, Paige left the room.

Downstairs again, she followed an arching passage that led to the back of the house. Long windows with black shutters gave tantalising glimpses of the view, the sails of a yacht on the horizon looking like a painting on a blue, blue canvas. She could see the pool, too, and its rippling surface revealed that someone was swimming laps. But it was impossible to see who it was, and, reaching the sun-drenched garden room that opened out onto the patio, she decided she would soon find out.

It was Sophie. As Paige crossed the patio and descended

to the tiled apron that surrounded the pool, her sister saw
her and swam to the side. Her curly blonde hair was dark
with moisture, which was why Paige hadn't recognised her,
and she was wearing a string bikini that Paige hadn't seen
before.

'Coming in?' she asked, resting her elbows on the rim.

Paige shook her head. 'Where is everyone?' she asked,
looking around. There was no sign of Nikolas or his ward.
The table where they had sat at breakfast was deserted, and
she was uneasily aware that she really knew next to nothing
about their relationship.

'Your boss said he had some work to do,' answered
Sophie carelessly, her fingers playing with the three gold
circles that defined the shape of her ear. 'I don't know
where the black widow is.'

'Sophie!' Paige sighed. 'In any case, you can hardly call
her that this morning. She's all in white.'

'She's still a pain,' muttered Sophie unrepentantly. 'Anyway, she disappeared soon after Petronides did. She's probably keeping out of the way, hoping we'll go away.'

Paige didn't say anything, but she suspected that Sophie
had a point. Ariadne wasn't going to make things easy for
them, and she dreaded what the girl would be like once
Nikolas wasn't here to chastise her.

'So—why don't you come for a swim?' asked Sophie
practically.

'Because I've just had a shower,' replied Paige, looking
uncertainly about her again. 'I wonder if the housekeeper
knows where she is?'

'Who cares?' Sophie pushed herself away from the wall
and turned a backward somersault. She came up streaming
with water, and wiped her eyes with the back of her hand
before going on, 'We might as well enjoy it while we can.
It's sort of like a holiday. And something tells me that
Madame Ariadne isn't going to let us enjoy it for long.'

Although Paige had been thinking the same thing herself,

she refused to believe it. 'She can't stop us,' she said, and Sophie groped for the side and looked up at her with suspicious eyes.

'You sound very sure,' she remarked. 'What do you know that you're not telling me?'

'Look, Ariadne didn't employ me; her guardian did,' replied Paige shortly. 'I'll leave here when he tells me to and not before.'

Sophie's eyes narrowed. 'You like him, don't you?'

'What I know of him.' Paige refused to be diverted. 'As employers go, he's all right, I suppose.'

'I don't mean that, and you know it,' retorted Sophie, watching her closely. She gave a short laugh. 'I don't believe it. After what you said to me, you're stuck on him yourself!'

'That's not true—'

'Oh, right. And I'm Madonna's uncle! Come off it, Paige, you think you've got a chance.'

'I don't.' Paige was horrified. 'Just because he wasn't what you expected, don't shift your fantasies onto me.'

Sophie shrugged. 'He is sexy.'

'And you're not the first female to think so.'

'Well, you can't deny it.' Sophie's tongue circled her lips. 'I wonder what he's like in bed?'

'For God's sake!' Paige was half afraid someone might hear them. Voices carried over water, and the last thing she needed was for Nikolas to hear them talking about him. 'I'm going to sit on one of those loungers. You can join me when you've finished.'

'Wait.' Sophie pulled herself up onto the rim of the swimming pool. 'What had you been doing? Earlier on, I mean. Why did you suddenly need another shower? I assume you had one as soon as you got up.'

'I did.' Paige was uncomfortable with the explanation. 'I'd been for a walk, that's all. But it was very hot and I wanted to get out of my shirt and shorts. They were sweaty.'

'A walk?' Sophie looked up at her enquiringly. 'Where did you walk to? Were you on your own?'

'No, I was with Mr Petronides,' answered Paige shortly, realising there was no point in lying about it when Nikolas could just as easily tell her himself. 'We walked as far as the cliffs, but unfortunately I got a headache. As I said, it was very hot so we came back.'

'I see.'

But Sophie's expression was provocative now and Paige lost her patience. 'Don't look at me like that,' she said. 'I was going alone but he saw me and decided to take the opportunity to talk to me about the job. Don't imagine that if you embarrass me enough I'll change my mind about staying here. I've accepted this position, and I'm going to do it to the best of my ability.'

'Big deal.' Sophie looked a little less pleased with herself now. 'And what am I supposed to do while you're doing your job?'

'You seemed to be having a good time when I came down,' Paige reminded her drily. 'Look, it's too hot to argue. Why don't you finish your swim?'

Paige was just beginning to wish she'd brought some sunscreen cream when she heard the unmistakable sound of footsteps behind her. For a moment, she thought it might be Nikolas, but when she turned her head she saw Ariadne trudging with evident reluctance towards her.

'Oh—hi,' she called, deciding it was up to her to try and get the girl to talk to her. 'Are you coming to join us?'

Ariadne looked as if she would have liked to turn around and go back into the house but she didn't. Despite her unwillingness to accept Paige as a friend, she had apparently been directed to make the best of it, and, after trailing down the steps, she positioned herself on another of the sunbeds, and opened the book she'd brought with her.

Paige compressed her lips. So much for a change of heart, she thought. Then, determined to make some headway, she asked, 'What are you reading?'

Ariadne turned the spine of the book up so that Paige could see it for herself, her eyes moving past her as she caught sight of Sophie in the pool. Her indignation was evident, and it didn't help that Sophie chose that moment to climb out onto the side. Wearing only the scanty bikini, she was clearly a source of irritation to the Greek girl, and Paige wondered if her sister was aware of how difficult she was making it for her.

Of course, she was. Sophie stood beside the pool, drying herself on one of the towels she'd taken from the stack on a table nearby. Then, as if she knew she was being watched, she bent and picked up her equally skimpy shorts, drawing them up over her damp legs with deliberate provocation.

Paige had to distract Ariadne, and, leaning forward, she said, 'Oh—you're reading *Jane Eyre*.' She'd recognised the author's name, not the title, but it was a fair guess that that was what it was. 'Are you enjoying it? I love the Brontë books.' She paused, seeking inspiration. 'Mr Rochester is such an attractive hero, don't you think?'

Ariadne pulled her hostile gaze back to her companion. 'Not as attractive as Nikolas,' she declared dispassionately. 'Don't you think Nikolas is attractive, Miss Tennant? So big, and dark, and powerful!'

Paige didn't know what to say. To deny it wasn't really an option, but, equally, to concede that she found him attractive would lay her open to all kinds of derision. Ariadne had already shown her contempt for the Englishwoman, and Paige had no desire to give her more ammunition for her arsenal.

'I'm not sure your guardian would approve of us discussing him,' she said at last. 'Um—have you read anything else by the Brontës? *Wuthering Heights*—that's by

Emily, of course—is very good, and Anne's novel, *The Tenant of Wildfell Hall*—'

'Don't you have a—how do you say?—a boyfriend, Miss Tennant?' Ariadne seemed determined to disconcert her. 'I am wondering how he feels about you spending several weeks away from home.'

Paige sighed, speculating on how far a companion was expected to go to satisfy the demands of her charge. 'Whether I have a boyfriend or not is no concern of yours, Ariadne,' she replied, keeping her tone pleasant with an effort. 'Now, perhaps we can talk about what you usually do when you're staying here. Do you swim? Go snorkelling? Ride?'

'Why are you so unwilling to talk about yourself, Miss Tennant?' countered Ariadne, without answering her. 'I shall begin to think you have something to hide.'

Paige expelled a weary breath. 'Why are you so determined to talk about me?' she retorted. 'I can't believe my history is of any interest to you whatsoever.'

'Oh, but you are wrong.' Ariadne laid her book aside and regarded her with bright, malicious eyes. 'I am curious as to why Nikolas would agree to bring both you and your sister to Skiapolis, when I clearly have no need of one companion, let alone two.'

Paige shrugged. 'Perhaps you should ask him,' she declared, looking up with some apprehension when a shadow fell across her. But it was only her sister.

'Ask who what?' asked Sophie irrepressibly, towelling the blonde tangle of her hair as she spoke. 'Let me guess: it has to be Nikolas. What's wrong? Is Ariadne showing her claws again?' She gave a derisive laugh. 'God, she's such a cliché!'

Ariadne's face darkened with anger. 'What? What are you saying? What did you call me?'

'I said you were a cliché,' replied Sophie carelessly, before Paige could stop her. 'You are. You're a sad case. Why don't you grow up?'

Ariadne gasped. 'I am—grown-up.'

'Yeah, right.' Sophie flopped down onto the nearest lounger and began drying her legs. 'I mean…' She stifled another giggle. 'Where did you get those clothes? Puhleeze!'

'There is nothing wrong with *my* clothes,' began Ariadne furiously, but Sophie wasn't even listening to her.

'Leggings!' she scoffed. 'Like they're still in style!' She looked at the other girl disparagingly. 'Come off it, Ari. Get a life!'

'Sophie!'

Paige was afraid she'd gone too far, but Ariadne was too agitated to notice. 'If—if you think *I* would wear what— what you are wearing—'

Her lips curled in disgust but Sophie wasn't offended. In the past six months she'd had to cope with much worse, and she was ready for her. 'You couldn't,' she retorted airily, lifting one leg and examining it with evident satisfaction. 'You don't have the figure for it.'

'There is nothing wrong with my figure.'

'What figure?' Sophie smirked. 'You say that enough times, you may just start believing it.'

Ariadne seethed. 'You—you are—insolent!'

'Yeah. Fun, isn't it?' Sophie stretched out on the lounger and crossed one ankle over the other. 'You know,' she added, glancing at Paige, 'I could get used to this.'

'You—you—'

Ariadne sprang to her feet, searching for a word to describe what she thought about the other girl at that moment, and then gave it up, and berated both of them in her own language. Her face was red and her hands trembled as she gesticulated her feelings, and for a moment Paige had visions of her attacking Sophie and both girls rolling about on the ground.

'Ariadne…' she protested, realising she had to say something to calm the situation, but it was too late. With a final imprecation, Ariadne charged away, her high-heeled sandals clattering noisily across the patio as she fled into the house.

The silence after she'd gone was almost deafening. And ominous, thought Paige gloomily. God knew what Ariadne was going to tell her guardian about this. It was all very well assuring herself that she couldn't be held responsible for her sister's behaviour, but the truth was she'd let her get away with it and she wasn't proud of herself for doing nothing to stop her.

Sophie had no such inhibitions. 'That's better,' she said. 'This place is half decent when she's not around. God, she's so boring! She acts more like seventy than seventeen.'

'All the same, you had no right to speak to her like that,' said Paige heavily. 'What she wears is nothing to do with you.'

'So what?' Sophie sniffed. 'It's time someone burst her bubble. She thinks she can say what she likes and no one's going to complain. Asking you whether you had a boyfriend, and why her old man invited both of us here. I mean—like that's anything to do with her.'

'He's not her old man.' Paige made the correction automatically. Then she realised what else Sophie had said. 'How do you know what we were talking about?'

'I've got ears.' Sophie was unrepentant. 'Sound carries around a pool, Paige; you know that. Anyway, you should be grateful I spoke up for you. You're too naïve. Being polite gets you nowhere with bitches like her. I know. I deal with them every day.'

Paige made an incredulous sound. 'I don't believe this. Sophie, we're not guests here. We're employees—or I am, anyway. And employees don't start throwing their weight around with their employers. I may be naïve, but I know that.'

'You also said that Ariadne wasn't your employer,' her sister reminded her shortly. 'Chill out, Paige. She's not likely to say anything, more's the pity.'

'What do you mean by that?'

'I mean, we're going to be stuck here no matter what,' muttered Sophie, brushing a fly away from her bare midriff. She grimaced. 'Still, I suppose it has its compensations. I'm looking forward to seeing what the ward-from-hell does when she realises she's got some competition.'

Paige gasped. 'That's ridiculous!'

'No, it's not. I've seen the way he looks at you.'

Paige couldn't help it; her face flamed with hot colour, and Sophie pointed at her triumphantly. 'You see!'

Paige got to her feet. 'I'm going to find Ariadne.'

'Why? Because you can't stand the heat?' Sophie arched a mocking brow.

'No, because I don't intend to sit here and listen to your nonsense any longer.'

'Okay.' Sophie shrugged. 'Have it your own way.' She glanced round. 'Would you mind moving that umbrella closer? I don't want to get burnt.'

Paige pursed her lips, but before she could tell the younger girl to do it herself Sophie spoke again.

'Hey, look who's here! Did I prick a nerve or what?'

Paige swung round, quite sure that this time it was Nikolas, coming to discipline Sophie, or, worse, to give them both notice, and caught her breath. Ariadne was walking back across the patio, the demure white outfit replaced by a cropped halter top in stripes of blue and yellow and a denim miniskirt that exposed the slender length of her legs. With her feet pushed into heel-less wedges, she looked young and pretty, and far different from the girl who had fled into the villa fifteen minutes before.

But her attitude didn't appear to have changed. Ignoring the two English girls, she subsided back onto the lounger she had occupied earlier, picking up her book and settling back against the cushions. Whether she was actually read-ing it or just using it as a means to avoid conversation, Paige couldn't be sure, but either way her own presence seemed superfluous.

'I'll see you later,' she said flatly, speaking mainly to Sophie. 'If you see Mr Petronides, tell him I've gone to finish my unpacking.'

Sophie propped herself up on her elbows. 'And what am I supposed to do with her?' She jerked a thumb in Ariadne's direction.

'Just—be civil,' said Paige wearily, realising that was probably impossible for her. 'I shan't be long.'

# CHAPTER SIX

PAIGE didn't see Nikolas again that day.

He didn't appear for lunch, which she and the two girls shared at the table on the patio, and afterwards Ariadne declared that she was going to take a rest. Paige guessed the girl was still recovering from the series of infections that had kept her away from school during the past term, and in all honesty she was tempted to do the same. She was tired, too, after the restless night she'd had, but she reminded herself again that she was not a guest here, and employees did not take time off when it suited them.

In consequence, she and Sophie spent the afternoon beside the pool. She even took a swim in the late afternoon, when the shadows were lengthening and the water in the pool was deliciously warm from the heat of the sun. Pleasantly tired, she took a shower before getting ready for dinner, quelling the unwanted sense of excitement she felt at the prospect of seeing their host again.

She needn't have worried. Nikolas didn't join them for dinner either. Kiria Papandreiu conveyed the news that Kirie Petronides was dining elsewhere this evening. Paige had great difficulty understanding her, but the phrase *'Then ineh etho!'* or 'He's out!' was familiar to her. Evidently, Nikolas did not consider it necessary to entertain them this evening. He'd apparently left that to Ariadne, who arrived rather later than was polite wearing the same resentful expression she had worn earlier.

But this evening Paige had no intention of allowing the younger girl to get the upper hand. Whatever Nikolas had had in mind when he'd brought her here, she couldn't believe he expected her to put up with Ariadne's insolence.

But she did wish her position had been more thoroughly defined.

'You have caught the sun, Miss Tennant,' Ariadne remarked somewhat smugly as she took her seat. 'It was very unwise to spend all afternoon beside the pool.'

'It was very pleasant,' replied Paige, helping herself to stuffed olives, endeavouring not to be aggravated by the girl's mocking tone. 'Are you feeling better?' she added, playing her at her own game. 'You looked rather pale when you went to take your rest.'

Ariadne's lips tightened. 'I'm perfectly all right.'

'Are you?' Paige regarded her without conviction. 'But your guardian told me you'd been ill. That's why he wants you to spend the summer here on the island.'

'That's not the reason,' said Ariadne crossly, and Paige was reminded of the argument the young girl had had with her guardian that morning. She could almost find it in her heart to feel sorry for Nikolas. It couldn't be easy for him dealing with someone of Ariadne's fiery temperament.

'Whatever,' she murmured now, and Sophie chose to intervene.

'Well, I think Ariadne would have much more fun in Athens,' she observed, following her own agenda. 'The island's okay, but it's dull. There's nothing going on.'

'What would you know?' enquired Ariadne sharply, and Paige could see another confrontation in the offing. It was apparently all right for the Greek girl to object to staying here, but, like any territorial animal, she defended her own.

'More than you, evidently,' began Sophie, always ready with an answer, but once again Paige cut her off.

'It doesn't really matter, does it?' she declared. 'We're all staying here for the summer. I suggest we try and make the best of it. It is a beautiful place.'

'Like the Garden of Eden,' said Sophie provokingly. 'And, like all earthly paradises, there has to be a serpent.'

'Are you implying—?'

'Where did you live before your parents died?' Paige broke in swiftly, not entirely sure that it was a suitable topic, but desperate to distract the girl from what Sophie had said.

'In Athens, of course.' To her relief, Ariadne chose to boast about it. 'My father had a huge villa not far from Nikolas's house there. That's how I know him so well.'

Paige inclined her head, acknowledging the explanation. 'And you went to school there, too?'

'Does it matter?' Ariadne was impatient now. 'I shall be leaving school very shortly. I'm almost eighteen, you know.'

Paige did know, and it was difficult to make conversation with someone who was so determined to be objectionable. Everything the Greek girl said was designed to provoke her and it was very hard not to let her succeed.

However, when Ariadne turned her frustration on one of the young maids, Paige felt obliged to say something in the young woman's defence. 'If you don't want any meat, Ariadne, don't have any,' she advised her shortly. 'Don't take your grievances out on innocent people, just because you've got a grudge against the world.'

Ariadne's jaw dropped. 'I don't know what you're talking about.'

'Yes, you do.' Paige was succinct. 'You've worn a sulky expression ever since we arrived. Well, I'm tired of sustaining this one-sided relationship. Where I come from, people treat each other with respect. I suggest you learn to do the same.'

Ariadne gasped. 'You can't speak to me like that.'

'I just did.'

'I'll tell Nikolas.'

'Go ahead. I doubt if he'd approve of your attitude either.'

Ariadne's nostrils flared. 'You know nothing about

Nikolas!' she exclaimed, and for once Paige was too angry to be discreet.

'More than you might imagine,' she declared crisply, realising belatedly that Sophie was listening to their exchange, too. 'Now, let's get on with dinner, shall we?' She glanced warningly at her sister. 'Without any more sly remarks.'

Ariadne stared at her disbelievingly for a few seconds, and then she got abruptly to her feet. 'I don't have to listen to this. I'll ask Kiria Papandreiu to serve my meal in my room.'

'No, you won't.' Now that she'd committed herself Paige had no choice but to go on. 'If you leave this table, you won't have any dinner. Do you understand? Now, stop be-having like a child and sit down.'

It didn't work. Not that she'd really thought it would. With a gesture of indignation, Ariadne threw down her nap-kin and, pushing past the startled maid, she left the room.

'Hey, way to go, Paige!'

Sophie was delighted, but Paige found no relief in her sister's approval. With slumped shoulders, she was forced to acknowledge that the direct approach hadn't worked, and she wondered if it would be any easier after Nikolas left for Athens. She wasn't hopeful. The girl had a severe case of bad attitude, and Paige suspected it would take more than her guardian's departure to alter her mood.

By the next morning, Paige had managed to shelve her own feelings of depression. This had to work. Somehow, some way, she had to gain Ariadne's confidence, and, de-ciding that the first thing she had to do was talk to Nikolas, she went down to the patio, hoping he and Ariadne might be having breakfast together.

But, although the table was laid for four, there was no one about. Paige propped her hands on her hips and stared somewhat uncertainly about her, wondering if Nikolas was up yet. It was typical that the previous day, when she hadn't been looking for him, he'd been there, whereas now…

'*Tha thelateh pro-ino, kiria?*'

Paige had to applaud the housekeeper's assiduity. She hadn't been aware that anyone had noticed her arrival, but they obviously had and now Kiria Papandreiu was asking her if she would like breakfast. 'Um—*kati elafro, efharisto*,' she murmured, dredging up the words from her small knowledge of the language. 'Just something light, thank you.'

'*Ne, kiria.*'

The old woman nodded and went away again, and Paige was relieved to find that she'd understood her. Deciding she might as well sit down while she waited, she seated herself at the table and gazed out towards the hazy line of the horizon. It was another beautiful day, and, she hoped, a more successful one.

A maid brought her warm rolls and orange juice and a steaming pot of coffee. And, because she'd eaten little after Ariadne had stormed out on them the night before, she ate three rolls, spread with some of the rich sweet conserve she found in the bread basket. Then, fortified with two cups of strong black coffee, she asked the maid to tell Kirie Petronides—if he asked—that she had gone for a walk.

She had intended just to go as far as the cliffs, but the beach looked so inviting, she couldn't resist it. She had no headache this morning, and although she wanted to speak to Nikolas she'd found she couldn't just sit meekly waiting for him to put in an appearance on the patio. Besides, it was still only just eight o'clock, and she had no idea what time he'd got home the night before.

Or where he'd been, she conceded as she descended the cliff steps. Not that it was any concern of hers. But she had thought he would stick around until Ariadne had learned to accept the situation. He knew what a sulky little madam she could be, and that was what Paige wanted to talk to him about. She wanted to know how much authority—or how little—she was expected to exert.

It was cooler on the beach. Kicking off her shoes, she curled her toes into the sand, enjoying the sensation of the grains sliding between her toes. She found if she walked in the shadow of the cliffs she could pretend she was back in England, walking along the sands at Bournemouth. When she was a little girl, her father had used to take his family to Bournemouth for two weeks every August, and she and Sophie, who had been little more than a toddler, had spent hours digging sandcastles and trying unsuccessfully to make a moat.

Of course, her mother had been alive then, and her father hadn't been so stressed about making a success of Tennants. He'd enjoyed his life in those days; they all had. It was only after her mother died that he'd turned all his energies into more and more reckless schemes to make money.

For the first couple of years, she'd been happy to support him. She'd been glad he'd had something to distract him from her mother's loss. She'd done whatever he'd asked of her, even to the extent of making herself pleasant to those of his business colleagues who needed the encouragement of being seen with a young and moderately attractive young woman to persuade them to part with their money.

And then he'd introduced her to Nikolas Petronides...

They'd been at a party in Monte Carlo at the time. Her father had been attending a seminar being run by a consortium of European financiers, and the Greek shipping magnate had posed a challenge he couldn't resist.

For some time, Parker Tennant had been trying to offload shares in a merchant shipping line that she'd later discovered had been in financial difficulties. Her father had invested his clients' money rather heavily in the enterprise, and he was looking for someone who might be willing to spend some of their own money to turn the company around.

Or, at least, that was what he'd told his daughter.

And she'd believed him.

Paige's lips twisted ruefully. She knew now it had all been a lie. Even before Nikolas had accused her of being a party to her father's scheme, she'd learned exactly how hollow Parker Tennant's promises were. In the years that followed, she'd lost count of the number of times he'd assured her that this time he was going to make a killing, only to find himself at the end of the day even deeper in debt. By the time he'd died, he'd owed a small fortune, and Paige had been left to salvage what she could from the wreckage.

Which was why Sophie was so bitter; why Paige couldn't altogether blame her sister when she did something outrageous. She was only following in the family tradition, after all. Goodness knew, Paige had made enough mistakes in her life.

But she'd never agreed to take part in any business negotiations after the affair with Nikolas. Whatever the truth was, he'd hurt her badly, and she'd had no intention of putting her heart on the line again.

Which was how she'd become involved with Martin Price.

She couldn't honestly say that she'd fallen in love with him as she had with Nikolas. Their relationship had been based on a mutual liking for one another, and she'd had no idea that Martin had a hidden agenda. She'd been so delighted to find someone who had no apparent connection to her father that she'd taken everything he said at face value, only learning the truth when the rest of her world was falling apart. In his own way, Martin had been just as ambitious as her father, and just as ruthless when things didn't go his way.

She sighed. That was all in the past now, and there was

no doubt that since meeting Nikolas again she'd realised how shallow her relationship with Martin had been. The affection she'd felt towards him had barely brushed the surface of the passion she'd shared with Nikolas, and a lump came into her throat at the thought of what she'd lost.

Feeling chilled, as much by her emotions as by the shadows cast by the cliffs, she walked out into the sunlight, going down the beach to the wooden jetty that jutted out into the water. Climbing onto it, she walked along, peering down into water that was so clear, she could see the many colourful fish swimming beneath its surface.

She didn't know what caused her to look back, but when she did she saw Nikolas strolling across the sands towards her. Either Kiria Papandreiu had given him her message and he'd come looking for her, or he'd had the same thought; she couldn't be sure. But as he got closer she saw the snorkelling mask dangling from his hand.

'Good morning,' he said as she reached the end of the jetty. 'I thought I might find you here.'

Paige forced a polite smile. 'You got my message, then,' she murmured, looking away from the searching warmth of his dark gaze. In an open-necked green shirt and black shorts, he was far too familiar. After the thoughts she'd been having, it would have been safer if they'd met up at the house.

'I saw Kiria Papandreiu, *ne*,' he agreed as she pretended to be looking at the fish. He paused. 'I see you find our wildlife fascinating. Perhaps you'd like to join me?'

'Join you?'

She looked up then, and he held up the masks so that she could now see he'd brought two. 'Why not?' he asked. 'I'm sure you'd enjoy it. It's early yet. I doubt if the girls are even up.'

Paige shook her head as if to clear it. 'I—as a matter of fact, I'd like to talk to you about Ariadne,' she said, glad of the opening he'd given her. 'I had hoped to speak to you yesterday, but, as I didn't, perhaps we could discuss my duties now.'

Nikolas's expression sobered. 'Your duties?' he queried. 'Or perhaps how I expect you to deal with Ariadne's attitude?' He frowned. 'She has told me you have been—what would you say?—short with her, *ohi*? I know it is not easy for you to believe, but she is a very insecure little girl.'

'But that's the point—she's not a little girl,' retorted Paige at once, stung at the thought of the two of them discussing her behaviour behind her back. 'And it's going to be useless if you countermand every instruction I give her. Last night, at dinner, she was especially—awkward. You said she needed a companion. In my opinion, she needs something more than that.'

Nikolas's mouth compressed. 'Did I say I had countermanded your instructions?' His eyes darkened, and she was intensely conscious of the fact that it was only because he was still standing on the sand that she was on a level with him. 'All I am saying is that appearances can be deceptive. She may seem very confident to you, but underneath she is crying out for—affection.'

Paige's lips tightened. 'Well, you'd know that better than me.'

Nikolas stepped up onto the jetty. 'What is that supposed to mean?'

His tone was harsher than before, and she was suddenly aware of her own insecurities. 'Just that affection is the last thing she'd ever want from me.'

'You think so?'

'Don't you?'

'Perhaps I am not the best person to judge,' he responded coolly. 'In your eyes, at least, my opinion does not count for very much.'

Paige had the feeling that they were getting off the subject. And, what was more, into deeper waters, figuratively speaking, than she wanted to go. It was difficult to keep her mind focussed on what she'd wanted to talk to him about when he persisted in turning the argument against her. She was also aware that she was sweating, and that she wasn't wearing a bra.

'Look, perhaps we can talk about this later,' she said, wondering if she could get past him without touching his lean frame. He was far more disturbing in casual clothes than he'd been in the more formal clothes he'd worn the day before, and defining her position as far as Ariadne was concerned did not seem half as important as getting away from him.

'You're nervous,' he said, disconcerting her still further. 'Surely I do not intimidate you?'

'Whether you intimidate me or not is hardly relevant,' retorted Paige tightly. 'As far as Ariadne is concerned, we must agree to differ. I'll keep what you say in mind, but I can't promise that she'll cooperate.'

Nikolas sighed. 'For what it's worth, I'll trust your judgement,' he said. 'Now—what's your decision?'

'My decision?' Paige's mind was blank. 'My decision about what?'

'About joining me for a swim,' he prompted, success-fully blocking the end of the jetty. He unbuttoned his shirt as he spoke, exposing the V of coarse hair that arrowed down below the waistband of his shorts. 'Come on. You'll enjoy it.'

Paige found that she was embarrassed by his suggestion. 'I don't think so,' she said stiffly. And then, remembering their changed relationship, she added, 'Thank you.'

'Why not?'

'Why not?' She swallowed. 'I think you know the an-swer to that as well as me. If you'll excuse me, I'll just go and see what Sophie is—'

'You're concerned because you don't have a swimsuit,' he remarked drily. 'So? I have seen you naked before.'

He would bring that up! Paige felt the blush of heat all

over her body. But she had to stop this, and stop it now, before he made a complete fool of her.

'I don't want to go swimming,' she said, refusing to submit to his blackmail. 'It's getting very hot. I'd rather go back to the house.'

'It's cooler in the water,' remarked Nikolas softly, and she was irresistibly reminded of how soft the water would feel against her hot skin. Her hot, *bare* skin, she recalled, avoiding the dark sensuality of his muscled flesh. 'Have you become a prude, *aghapita*? Surely you know that no one but I can see you here?'

Paige breathed shallowly. 'That's not the point.'

'So what is the point, *pirazi*?'

Inspiration came to her. 'I'm your employee. Not your guest.'

Nikolas lifted his shoulders. 'I do not believe that bothers you.'

'It should bother you.'

'And if it does not?'

'It would bother Ariadne,' said Paige childishly, and it was only when his eyes narrowed that she realised she had said the wrong thing.

'So?' He moved towards her and, because there was nowhere to go but off the end of the jetty, she was forced to stay where she was. 'You are jealous, Paige.' His hand cupped her nape, and she steeled herself against his mocking appraisal. 'You would like to go swimming with me, but you're afraid of upsetting that stubborn little streak you call a conscience, *ohi*?'

'No!' She was horrified at his perception. 'I just see no point in raking up the past. And besides, you're only having fun at my expense. What do you really want, Nikolas? Flesh? Or blood?'

'I want…' His thumb brushed the corner of her mouth, and she bit her lip to prevent its sensual invasion. 'Oh, there are many things I want, Paige.' He looked down at her breasts, which were taut and swollen against the thin cotton of her shirt. His lips twisted. 'And you naked is not on my agenda.'

Paige held up her head. 'I'm—I'm pleased to hear it.'

'Are you? Are you really?' He moved even closer and his powerful thigh brushed against her own. His breath fanned her temple. 'So I'm not disturbing you? Not even a little? Knowing that we're here and completely alone doesn't bother you at all?'

Paige moved her neck against his fingers. 'Should it?' she managed at last, striving for indifference, and at last she succeeded in provoking him.

'*Hristo*, it bothers me,' he bit out savagely, his fingers tight on her shoulders now. And then his mouth was on hers, and his tongue allowed no resistance as it thrust between her lips.

If it had been a game on his part, it had backfired. When he kissed her, she knew instantly that what he was doing was beyond his control. But then, it was beyond hers, too, and she clutched dizzily for his arm to prevent herself from tumbling backwards into the water. For a few mindless minutes, she was too bemused to think of anything but him, anything but the searing heat of his mouth.

Then she was in his arms, close against the urgent demands of his body, aware of the violent reaction he was having towards her that he wasn't even trying to disguise. Not that he could, she thought unsteadily, imagining how she would feel if he pulled her down onto the sun-warmed slats beneath them. How hot and heavy *he'd* feel, pressing her to the jetty, how hot and heavy and hard his arousal would feel sliding into her wet sheath...

She opened her legs almost instinctively, wanting him to touch her, wanting him to know how aroused she was. But instead of slipping his hand beneath her hem he thrust her away from him, a superhuman effort that left him swaying and red in the face.

'*Exipnos*, Paige,' he muttered. '*Poli exipnos*. Clever. Very clever.'

And, without giving her a chance to defend herself, he tore off his shirt and dived cleanly into the water.

# CHAPTER SEVEN

PAIGE heard the helicopter as she was having a shower that evening. Now that she knew what it was, she had no difficulty in identifying the throbbing blades, and her nerves tightened at the realisation that Nikolas must have sent for it. Which probably meant he was leaving. But when? Tonight? Tomorrow? She expelled a painful breath. Soon.

She wasn't surprised. After what had happened that morning, he was unlikely to want to prolong his stay on the island. The wonder of it was that she hadn't been given her marching orders, too. She'd certainly expected it. She'd shamed him and she'd shamed herself and he was unlikely to forgive her for that.

Luckily Ariadne hadn't been about when she'd returned to the villa from the beach. She'd had time to go up to her room and compose herself before she'd been obliged to go down and face her responsibilities. And, although she was sure the girl must have wondered why she hadn't wanted anything but coffee, it apparently hadn't occurred to her that Paige might have been up earlier.

Besides, she'd been intent on convincing Paige that she was sorry for the way she'd behaved the night before. She'd made some excuse about letting Sophie upset her, and Paige had had to concede, to herself at least, that her job might have been easier without her sister's particular brand of provocation.

Whatever, by the time Nikolas had appeared, dark and unsmiling in a navy blue shirt and matching cotton trousers, his damp hair slicked back behind his ears, they'd been chatting together in comparative harmony. If the conversation had been slightly one-sided and Ariadne had chosen

...me to talk about her guardian and the things
...done together, Paige hadn't complained. She'd been
...relieved to find they could have a civil conversation,
and if the girl's words had sometimes scraped a nerve she'd
managed not to show it.

Nikolas's arrival, however, had disturbed Paige more
than she'd cared to admit. His brusque, *'Kalimera,'* issued
for Ariadne's benefit, she had no doubt, had done nothing
to reassure her, and his invitation to his ward to accompany
him on a trip he intended to make to the other side of the
island had left her feeling chilled and superfluous.

There had been no question of her going with them, and
after the exchange she'd had with Nikolas earlier she'd
been half prepared for him to issue her dismissal. He hadn't
then, but she'd spent the whole day in a state of extreme
agitation, and, of course, Sophie had assumed that Ariadne
had arranged the whole thing.

'Hey, don't let them get to you!' she'd exclaimed, while
they were having lunch together. Nikolas and his ward
hadn't returned, and Sophie thought Paige was worrying
that Ariadne might take the opportunity to complain about
her behaviour the night before. 'So what if she slags you
off to her old man?' she'd added carelessly. 'He's not going
to listen to anything she has to say. You've got to have
some authority. I thought you did good, myself.'

Paige had denied it, of course, consoling herself with the
thought that Nikolas was unlikely to discuss his real reasons
for firing her with either of the girls. If he did decide to
fire her. Whatever happened, she had only herself to blame.

But nothing had happened. Even though she'd been sitting on the patio when they'd arrived home, no one had
disturbed her. She'd heard the scrape of the car's tyres as
they'd swept across the gravel, listened to the sound of
footsteps crossing the entrance hall, felt her skin prickle
with the awareness that Nikolas was back, but that was all.
Eventually, she'd had to come upstairs to change for dinner

without any idea of where Nikolas was or what he planned to do.

Standing in front of her mirror now, fastening her bra, she endeavoured to think positively about the evening ahead. If Nikolas could treat her with indifference, she should be able to do the same. If only...

She sighed. Perhaps it would be easier if she took the initiative and told him she was leaving. Simpler, certainly, she reflected bitterly, viewing her mini-brief-clad hips without liking. It would obviously remove all the uncertainty from her position, but then she'd be forced to go back to London and face all the problems she'd left there.

She groaned. When had her life become so complicated? When her father had died? When Martin had arranged for her to meet Nikolas again? Or four years ago, when she'd walked into a cocktail party and fallen in love with a man whose only interest in her had been sexual?

She started when the door behind her opened suddenly. Sophie sauntered carelessly into the room, but although she was relieved Paige was in no mood to treat her sister with her usual tact.

'Can't you knock?' she exclaimed, snatching up the long-sleeved black knit she was planning to wear for dinner and holding it to her chest. 'I'd prefer a little privacy, if you don't mind.'

'Tough!' Sophie dismissed her feelings as if they were of no account. 'Don't take it out on me because you can't cut it. I've told you. You've got nothing to worry about.'

Paige wished she could be as confident. Changing tack, she said, 'You're not planning on going down to dinner in that outfit, are you?'

'Why? What's wrong with it?' Sophie regarded her thin cropped vest and lacy miniskirt with obvious satisfaction. 'Chill out, can't you? I look okay.'

'You look—tarty,' said Paige, deciding she was running

the risk of creasing her own dress and wriggling into it.
'I'd have thought you'd want to look your age, at least.'

Sophie pulled a face. 'That's not going to work, Paige.'
She admired the stud she'd put into her nose this evening
and scowled at her reflection. 'Think again.'

Paige shook her head. The piercing of Sophie's nostril
had been a bone of contention between them weeks before
the marijuana incident, and she had hoped she'd persuaded
her not to wear the stud again. But evidently this evening
her sister was looking for trouble, and Paige was too weary
to start another argument.

'So what do you want?' she asked, picking up her brush
and tugging it through her honey-gold bob.

'Some excitement. Somebody interesting to talk to. A
*joint*!' Sophie emphasised the final demand with defiance.
'Do I have to have a reason for coming into your room? I
thought you might be glad of my support.'

*Her support?* Paige couldn't believe she'd said that.
Shaking her head, she said ruefully, 'Not dressed like that.'

'Then stuff you!' said Sophie rudely, striding back to the
door. She jerked it open and then turned to regard her sister
with a mocking gaze. 'You can tell your precious employer
that I'm not hungry.' Her lips twisted. 'Oh, and by the way,
your bum does look big in that!'

With a grimace of satisfaction, she slammed the door
behind her. Paige was tempted to go after her, but she knew
it wouldn't do any good. In this mood, Sophie was unlikely
to listen to anything she had to say, and it was a bit late to
wish she hadn't been so negative about her clothes. That
dig about wanting a 'joint' was worrying, and it was only
the fact that she knew she couldn't get into any trouble
here that persuaded her to abandon the problem.

She sighed. It was time she was going downstairs. She
wasn't looking forward to it, but she didn't have a choice.
Besides, if it was at all possible, she had to try and repair
the damage she'd done that morning. If Nikolas was leav-

ing, he might have decided to give her a second chance. She could only hope so.

Despite her best efforts, her nose had caught the sun, and she used a blocking cream to disguise its redness. Then, after darkening her lids with eyeshadow and smoothing a beige lip gloss over her generous mouth, she was ready. Or as ready as she'd ever be, she thought ruefully. She just hoped Ariadne was still in a good mood.

Her heeled sandals announced her progress as she went downstairs, and as no one came to meet her she walked purposefully towards the room where they'd gathered for drinks the night Nikolas had dined at home.

She paused uncertainly in the doorway at the sight of a strange man helping himself to a drink from the cabinet. He wasn't as tall as Nikolas, but he was equally dark, with a stocky build and hair that appeared to be receding from a high forehead. There was no sign of Ariadne or her guardian, however, and Paige allowed a small sigh to escape her. What now?

'*Kalispera*, Miss Tennant.'

She'd turned to look back towards the stairs when the man spoke, and she swung round again in some confusion. 'I'm sorry. Do I know—? Yanis!' She realised suddenly who he was. 'Yanis Stouros. I didn't recognise you.'

'*Then pirazi.*' Yanis smiled. 'It doesn't matter, *kiria*. We are all getting older. I've put on a little weight, and my hair—' He ran a rueful hand over his scalp, before coming towards her to grasp her outstretched fingers. 'It's good to see you again. Are you well?'

'I—I'm fine.' Paige let him enclose her hands with his. 'I didn't realise you were here. Where have you been hiding yourself?'

'I only arrived a short time ago,' he explained warmly, and she remembered the helicopter she had heard earlier. 'But I hear you are now working for Nikolas. We are both—what is that expression you use?—in the same boat, *ohi*?'

Paige managed a thin smile. 'Is that what he told you?'

'No.' Yanis shrugged. 'He told me you are here to make a friend of Ariadne. That is good. She needs female companionship. The little one is too much on her own.'

'Is she?' Paige reserved judgement. She was fairly sure that Ariadne wouldn't agree with him, despite their conversation that morning. And as for calling Ariadne 'the little one'—Paige felt a rueful disbelief. The girl had evidently wrapped both men round her little finger. 'Well, we'll see,' she added determinedly. 'I'm not sure how it's going to work out.'

Yanis's smile gentled. 'Do not let her—give you the hard time,' he urged softly. 'Ariadne can be wilful, I know, but she means well. And you have Nikolas's confidence. Remember that.'

*Do I?*

This time Paige kept the comment to herself, but she suspected from his expression that Yanis knew exactly what she was thinking. 'So,' she murmured, changing the subject, 'how are you?' She looked down at his blunt-fingered hands still clasping hers. 'You're not married?'

'Who would have me?'

Yanis pulled a wry face, but his eyes were intent on hers and she remembered how kind he'd been to her when her relationship with Nikolas had ended. But she didn't want his admiration. Particularly as any mistakes she'd made now were peculiarly her own.

'I'm sure that isn't a problem,' she said hurriedly, aware that somehow their conversation had become too personal. Her fault, probably. She should never have made that reference about him not being married. What he did or didn't do was nothing to do with her. She took another breath. 'Um—where's Nikolas?'

'I'm here.'

Paige was startled. As always, Nikolas had found a way to disconcert her, and the realisation that he was standing right behind her now caused an uneasy fluttering in her stomach. She couldn't help wondering how long he'd been there and what interpretation he'd put on her exchange with Yanis. The two men were much of an age and she hoped he didn't imagine she'd been flirting with his assistant.

'Let me get you a drink, *kiria*.' Yanis found a way to ease her misgivings and Paige was glad of his intervention. She stepped further into the room, allowing Nikolas to move past her, and the two men approached the drinks cabinet together.

'Miss Tennant prefers wine,' Nikolas remarked as he joined his assistant, and Paige thought how elegant he looked this evening. In a cream shirt and black trousers, a tissue-thin black leather jacket accentuating the width of his shoulders, he was more formally dressed than usual, and Paige wondered tensely if he was leaving tonight. It was possible he had a dinner engagement in Athens, and her pulse quickened at the thought that he might be meeting some other woman. She was struggling to come to terms with how she felt about this possibility when he added, 'Am I not right?'

'What?' She couldn't think what he was talking about and, although she'd been avoiding his eyes, now she was caught and held by his sardonic gaze. 'Oh—the wine. Y-yes,' she stammered as a latent comprehension dawned. 'Thank you.'

'*Efharistisi mou,*' he replied politely, turning back to Yanis, and Paige's hand sought the gold chain that circled her throat almost protectively.

Obviously he'd had time to put what had happened that morning into perspective, she decided bleakly. The cold detachment he'd exhibited earlier had disappeared, or perhaps the presence of Yanis had mellowed his mood. Either way, the fears she'd been stressing over all day seemed to have been unfounded. Unless he intended to wait until after dinner to deliver his ultimatum.

Whatever, she determined not to feel threatened by his ability to act like a chameleon. If her past experience had taught her anything it was that men rarely put their true feelings on display. No matter how uncertain she might feel, she had to behave as if nothing had happened, as if being in the same room as Nikolas didn't shred what little composure she had left.

She turned deliberately to Yanis. 'Did you fly in from Athens?' she asked, and he stepped forward to hand her a glass of white wine.

'*Sosta,*' he agreed. 'That's right.' He lifted his own glass of retsina in a silent salute to her. 'Regrettably, it is to be a short visit. We have to return to the office tomorrow.'

'Tomorrow?' Paige knew she sounded dismayed, but she couldn't help it. 'So soon.'

'But it is the reason you are here, is it not?' enquired Nikolas, moving to stand between them. 'It is the reason I employed you. You are not having second thoughts, are you, Paige?'

Paige took a deep breath. 'Are you?'

It was a gamble, asking him outright, and Nikolas's eyes darkened with sudden emotion. 'My feelings are not in question here,' he declared. 'I offered you the job. However…' he paused, and her nerves stretched endlessly '…if the situation is not to your liking, I can always look for someone else.'

Paige felt a tremor deep inside her. 'If you have confidence in my abilities, I'm prepared to continue,' she said, aware that Yanis was watching their exchange with sudden interest. 'You're happy with the way Ariadne responds to me? You have no complaints about her treatment at my hands?'

'You make yourself sound like a—how do you put it?

A termagant, *ohi*?' Nikolas mocked her. 'You are not so tough.'

She wasn't. But she resented him commenting on the fact. 'Don't be fooled,' she said tersely. 'I can be quite tough when I want to be. Appearances can be deceptive, you know.'

'I do know,' he said harshly, and then, as if remembering they were not alone, he turned abruptly away. 'Where is Ariadne? And your sister? Surely they know what time dinner is served?'

'Um—Sophie won't be joining us,' said Paige awkwardly. Conversely now, she wished she was, miniskirt and all. 'She—er—she says she's not hungry.'

'That's a shame.' It was Yanis who spoke. 'I would have liked to meet her. She is younger than you, I think.' His eyes twinkled. 'But not so beautiful, *isos*?'

'She is skin and bone,' retorted Nikolas, before Paige could say anything in Sophie's defence. He scowled. 'At least Paige does not appear to be starving herself to death.'

'In other words, I could lose some weight,' said Paige tersely. 'Thank you, Nikolas. That's just what a woman wants to hear.'

'That was not what I meant,' he snapped, his temper dangerously close to erupting. 'Oh—' He swore in his own language. 'Here is Ariadne; at last.'

It was just as well. Paige had the feeling that he no longer cared what Yanis thought. But she did. She had no desire for Nikolas's assistant to guess what had been going on. He would think she was a fool. And she was. But where Nikolas was concerned it was hard to be detached.

Ariadne had evidently decided to get dressed up this evening. Her short-skirted coral-pink dress was obviously new, its low neckline drawing attention to the smooth skin of her throat. She'd plaited her hair and wound it into a coronet, and pearl earrings dangled from her ears. She looked

older, and more sophisticated, and Paige saw Nikolas's
eyes widen with obvious pride and admiration.

'*Theos!*' he exclaimed, going to meet her. 'You look—'
He paused, and then added softly, 'Very beautiful.'

'Do you think so?' Ariadne preened herself, her dark
eyes caressing his lean figure. 'So do you.'

Nikolas's mouth thinned. 'Men do not look beautiful,
*pethi*,' he corrected her a little curtly, and Paige stiffened
when his gaze drifted briefly in her direction. 'But your
parents would have been proud of you. As I am. You look
so much like Leni did at the same age.'

Ariadne's lips tightened. 'You treat me like a child,
Nikolas.' She looked round as if seeking a scapegoat, and
then frowned. 'Where is Miss Tennant's sister?'

'Sophie is not joining us this evening,' replied her guardian smoothly. 'Miss Tennant says she is not hungry.
Perhaps she has had too much sun.'

'Oh.' Ariadne wasn't pleased. Paige could tell that. She'd
obviously hoped to impress the younger girl, however offhand she'd been towards her.

'I think she's tired,' Paige murmured placatingly, glancing ruefully at Yanis. Then she turned once more towards
the girl. 'I—er—I like your dress. It's very pretty.'

'Pretty!' Ariadne was clearly not impressed by her com-
pliment. 'Versace does not make pretty dresses, Miss
Tennant. They are works of art. Original creations of style
and design—'

'That is a Versace original?' Nikolas interrupted her. His
brows drew together in a way Paige knew well. 'When did
you—?'

'*Entaxi, entaxi!*' Ariadne's face had flushed with unbe-
coming colour. 'All right, all right. It belonged to my
mother, okay? There, are you satisfied now?'

'No, I am not satisfied, *thespinis*.' Nikolas's face was
bleak. 'Who gave you permission to riffle through your

mother's belongings? Who said you could wear Leni's clothes?'

'I don't need anyone's permission.' But Ariadne was looking less sure of herself now. 'They were just hanging there, in the closet in the house in Athens. They looked so beautiful, and so neglected. I thought you wouldn't mind if I brought some of them with me.'

Nikolas was breathing deeply. 'Do you not have anything suitable of your own to wear?'

'Of course I do.' Ariadne looked resentfully at Paige, as if she blamed her for this debacle. 'Oh, don't be cross with me, please, *aghapitos*. I wanted to look beautiful for you.'

'And you could not accomplish this without wearing your mother's dresses?' Nikolas was obviously controlling his temper, but his tone was hardly less remote. 'What nonsense is this when your closet is stuffed with—' He broke off and stifled an oath before continuing. 'We will speak of this later, Ariadne. You have embarrassed me in front of our guests.'

'You've embarrassed me—' protested Ariadne defensively, but then seemed to think better of it. Going up to her guardian, she laid her hand on his sleeve. 'I am sorry, Nikolas. Will you forgive me?'

Paige saw Nikolas hesitating, and she had to steel herself not to remind him of how rude the girl had been earlier. 'I will think about it,' he said, but it was obvious he was softening. 'Enough. Do you want a Coke? Or would you rather have some wine?'

'May I?'

Ariadne followed him across the room as he went to attend to her needs, but not before casting a rather malevolent look in Paige's direction. It was obvious she blamed her for bringing the matter up in the first place, and Paige's spirits drooped at the thought that this morning's progress might never have occurred.

Dinner was served on the terrace this evening. A table

had been laid beneath an awning and the delicious smell of barbecued meats greeted them as they stepped outside. It was already dark, but the terrace was illuminated by dozens of candles, their mellow light more subtle than the oil lamps that hung from the balcony.

The meal was served, buffet-style, from long tables which had been set up beside the pool. Paige guessed their situation was deliberate. It meant the waiters couldn't eavesdrop on their conversation.

Paige couldn't help but be impressed by the organisation that had gone into preparing the meal. As well as the lamb and pork that was roasting on the grills, the tables were spread with cold meats and salads, savoury eggs and stuffed tomatoes. There was swordfish, served with a Greek salad, and aubergines filled with a ragout of vegetables and herbs. And, to finish, a selection of rich puddings, served with ice cream or some of the delicious thick yoghurt that tasted nothing like the supermarket variety they got back home.

Paige decided it was lucky that she wasn't particularly hungry. With so many fattening things to choose from, she could easily add several inches to her hips. It was a pity Sophie wasn't here. Even she might have been tempted by the deep-fried doughnuts, dipped in honey syrup and sprinkled with cinnamon. Though, knowing her sister, it was unlikely she'd eat anything she couldn't count the calories of first.

Still, she would have liked her to meet Yanis. She had a soft spot in her heart for the man. He hadn't judged her as Nikolas had done. He'd realised her father had used her, too. It was he who'd arranged her flight back to London four years ago; who'd understood her need to get away.

'By the way, I am leaving in the morning, Ariadne,' Nikolas remarked casually as they were enjoying some of Kiria Papandreiu's strong black coffee after the meal. Until then, conversation had been light and impersonal, and Paige had been glad to concentrate on the food. 'Yanis and I have a morning meeting in Athens, and we'll be flying to Paris at the end of the week. But I should be able to spend the following weekend with you. So long as there are no unexpected problems, of course.'

'But that's almost two weeks!' Ariadne was horrified. 'And I have to stay here? On my own?'

'You are not staying here on your own. You have the company of Miss Tennant and her sister,' Nikolas reminded her crisply. 'I suggest you use the time to get to know one another.'

Ariadne hunched her shoulders. 'That's easy for you to say,' she muttered. 'When you're not here, I get bored.'

'Bored?' Yanis intervened. 'You must be joking. I wish I could stay here. Who wouldn't want to exchange the noise and pollution of the city for the peace and beauty of the island?'

'I would,' retorted Ariadne sulkily. 'I miss the city, Nikolas. I miss my friends.'

'You will have friends here,' said Nikolas, once again having to control his patience. 'Ariadne, I want you to build your strength up. I want you to play squash and tennis and to swim—'

'I am not an athlete,' declared Ariadne coldly. 'I like going shopping, going to the movies, eating out.'

'We have had this discussion before,' her guardian warned her curtly. 'I grow tired of it, and so, I would assume, does Miss Tennant. I suggest you make the best of it. Otherwise I may make other arrangements in the fall.'

Ariadne gazed at him. 'What do you mean? What other arrangements?'

'Another tutor, perhaps,' said Nikolas quellingly. 'If you are not completely well. It might even be an idea for you to be tutored here, on the island. As Yanis says, it is probably healthier for a growing girl.'

Ariadne caught her breath. 'You wouldn't do that.'

'If you push me far enough, I can be a formidable foe,'

replied her guardian, sipping the brandy he'd been served after the meal. 'What do you say?'

'I don't have a lot of choice, do I?' Ariadne blew out a breath and then got to her feet. 'May I be excused?' she asked, and Nikolas inclined his head in agreement.

'Goodnight, little one,' he said, his voice gentler, and Ariadne rounded the table to bestow a kiss on each of his dark cheeks. Whatever hostility there had been between them was evidently forgotten. Ariadne looked as smugly confident as ever when she left the room.

Conversely Paige felt awkward after the girl had gone. After all, she was only here to keep Ariadne company, not to socialise with her employer and his guests. Lifting her cup, she swallowed the remains of her coffee, but before she could make her escape Yanis spoke again.

'Young people,' he said, looking sympathetically at her. 'They always want to grow up too soon.'

Paige forced a smile. 'I think all teenagers are the same,' she murmured, grateful for his understanding. 'I know Sophie was just as awkward when she heard we were coming here.'

'Was she?' To her dismay, it was Nikolas who took her up on her words. 'You didn't tell me that.'

'Well…' Paige tried to be offhand. 'It wasn't relevant. I only mentioned it now to show that Ariadne isn't the only one to think that island life can be—can be boring.'

'Perhaps you think it is boring, also.' Nikolas's eyes had narrowed, and Paige gave an indignant sigh.

'Of course I don't,' she said. 'I was talking about Ariadne. And Sophie. In any case, my feelings are not in question here, are they?' she added, turning the words he had used to her back on him. 'Don't be so sensitive, Nikolas.'

Nikolas shrugged. 'Do you think I am too lenient with Ariadne?'

Paige shook her head. 'That's not for me to say.'

'So you do?'

'I didn't say that.'

'You didn't have to.' His tone was disparaging. 'I could see it in your expression when we were talking about the dress.'

She would have to be more careful, Paige thought as he helped himself to more brandy. He was far too perceptive where she was concerned. 'I wouldn't dream of questioning your behaviour,' she said at last, finishing her coffee. 'And now, if you'll excuse me also—'

'You're not going to bed?' Yanis was on the point of rising to go and get himself more coffee from the buffet table, but now he paused, his empty cup in his hand.

'I'm afraid so.' Paige was sorry to disappoint him, but she suspected Nikolas was taking his frustration with his ward out on her. 'It's been nice seeing you again, Yanis. I hope we'll meet again before too long.'

Yanis nodded. 'Sleep well,' he said. 'I shall look forward to seeing you again when I return. And meeting your sister, too. Give her my regards, won't you?'

'I will.'

As if sensing he was in the way now, Yanis went to get his coffee, but when Paige would have left her seat also Nikolas intervened. 'What do you think you are doing to me?' he demanded, his voice low and impassioned, his anger so unexpected that Paige sank back into her chair.

'I beg your pardon—?'

'You are baiting me,' he said harshly, leaning across the table towards her. 'Not content with making a fool of me this morning, you seek to humiliate me again tonight.'

'To humiliate you?' Paige's gaze was uncomprehending. 'I don't know what you're talking about,' she whispered, afraid that Yanis might overhear them. 'I wanted to apologise, as a matter of fact. What happened this morning—'

'*Nothing* happened this morning,' Nikolas broke in

grimly. 'Do not imagine for one moment that it meant anything to me.'

'I don't.' But she was paralysed by his fury. 'I hoped you'd forgotten it, actually. I—I've been trying to do the same.'

'I just bet you have.' Nikolas scowled, in no way appeased by her admission. 'Tell me, Paige: do you think this is a game we're playing?'

'A game?' Paige was confused. 'I don't understand. You're not making any sense.'

'Because I should warn you,' he added, 'there can only be one winner. Do you think you've got what it takes?'

# CHAPTER EIGHT

IT WAS after ten o'clock before Ariadne appeared the following morning.

Paige had been up before the helicopter took off, and although it flew out over the ocean she didn't know how anyone could sleep through it. But evidently Ariadne had, and Sophie, and she decided it must be because she was burdened with a conscience that she found it so difficult to rest. She seemed to have been in a state of turmoil ever since her father's death and nothing she did seemed to turn out the way she expected.

But today was a new day, she told herself firmly. Nikolas was gone and wouldn't be back for over a week, which was surely time enough for her to get some organisation into her life. By the time he returned, she wanted to be able to tell him that she had established a routine, and if that meant going head-to-head with his ward, then so be it.

Nevertheless, it was daunting when her charge chose not to put in an appearance until a quarter-past ten. Half the morning was over, and even Sophie had turned up to drink three cups of coffee and nibble on a slice of toast before taking up her position beside the pool. Their breakfast table had been cleared, and Paige hoped Ariadne didn't think she was going to spend another hour choosing what she wanted to eat.

In consequence, she was pacing the patio when the Greek girl sauntered out of the house. In a cropped vest and white shorts, her hair hanging in a long braid over one shoulder, she looked absurdly young and vulnerable, and Paige tempered her impatience with the thought that this couldn't be easy for Ariadne, having strangers living in the house.

101

'Good morning,' she said, pushing her own hands into the pockets of her navy skirt. 'Did you oversleep?'

Ariadne's eyes sparkled with momentary hostility, but then she said carelessly, 'I never get up early unless there's something I want to do.'

'Okay.' Paige weathered the barb without expression. 'So, you don't think there's anything to do.' She gestured towards the table. 'Do you want anything to eat, or is that something you don't consider important either?'

'Oh, I have had breakfast.' Ariadne cupped her hands around her eyes and gazed towards the pool. 'And, unlike your sister and yourself, I do not have to fry my flesh to give my skin some colour.'

Paige controlled her temper with difficulty. 'Do you ever say anything pleasant about anybody?' she asked, refusing to be provoked, and Ariadne shrugged.

'Of course,' she said, her hands falling to her sides. 'When it's warranted.' She heaved a sigh. 'I think I'll go and get my book—'

'No.' Paige broke in before she could finish the sentence, and Ariadne gazed at her in some surprise.

'No?' she echoed. 'I beg your pardon?'

'It's a simple word.' Paige regarded her steadily. 'I said, no. You will not go and get your book.'

Ariadne gasped. 'I will if I want to.'

'No, you won't.' Paige was getting into her stride. 'So long as your guardian's not here, I am responsible for your well-being, and despite what you told Nikolas I think some exercise will do you good.'

'If you think I'm going to waste time on those machines in the gym—'

'Who said anything about going to the gym?' Paige blew out a breath. 'I think a walk will suffice for this morning. But you can show me the gym later. I may wish to use it myself.'

Ariadne put her hands on her hips. 'Well, some of us

need exercise more than others,' she declared rudely, and Paige had to restrain the impulse to walk away.

'As you say,' she managed, apparently without taking umbrage. 'But as I'm in charge that's what we're going to do.'

Ariadne's jaw jutted. 'You can't make me.'

'D'you want to bet on it?' Paige's height and more statuesque build gave her some advantage, after all, and Ariadne glowered at her.

'I'm going to ring Nikolas tonight and tell him what you've said,' she muttered, but Paige wasn't alarmed. She'd been threatened by better people than Ariadne, she thought wryly. Nothing the girl said could hurt her as much as Nikolas's bitterness had done.

'Ring him, with pleasure,' she said carelessly. 'But be prepared for a less than favourable response. He employed me, remember? Your guardian has a great—respect—for my good judgement.'

And that was as far as she was prepared to go in defending herself, Paige decided firmly. She was still unconvinced about the reasons Nikolas had brought her here, and she couldn't entirely dismiss the notion that he was seeking some revenge.

Ariadne sniffed. 'I thought you got a headache when you went out in the sun.'

*You wish,* thought Paige drily, but she held her tongue. 'I'll survive,' she said instead. 'Shall we go?'

'What about—your sister?'

'Well, I'll ask her if she wants to join us, but don't hold your breath.' Paige pulled a wry face. 'Let's go.'

As she'd expected, Sophie insisted that she was going to swim laps as soon as her breakfast had been digested. And, although Paige was tempted to point out that coffee and dry toast needed little digesting, she didn't press her. She was determined to get Ariadne to talk to her, and she was unlikely to do that with Sophie picking on her at every opportunity.

'Where are we going?' asked Ariadne sulkily as Paige led the way through the gardens and into the shade of the fruit orchard. 'Not down to the beach!'

'Why not?'

Despite what had happened the day before, Paige did intend to go down to the beach. It would be cool beneath the cliffs, and she was hoping it would exorcise the images that had stuck in her mind.

'I hate the beach,' said Ariadne sullenly. 'I never go down there.'

Paige cast a disbelieving glance over her shoulder. 'You must do when you go swimming.'

'I swim in the pool,' declared Ariadne shortly. 'I hate the sand. It gets everywhere. In your hair, in your shoes—'

'Not if you take your shoes off,' replied Paige practically. 'I love the beach. I love the feeling of sand sliding between my toes.'

'You would.' Ariadne was disparaging.

'Yes, well—so will you if you stop behaving like a temperamental prima donna.' Paige shook her head. 'I can't believe you spend months of the year in a place like this without swimming in the sea. A pool is so—tame.' She frowned as another thought occurred to her. 'You can swim, I suppose?'

'Of course I can swim.' Ariadne was indignant. 'I'm not stupid, you know.'

'I never thought you were.' Paige gave a shrug. 'That's not your problem.'

'I do not have a problem.' Ariadne scowled. 'Did you tell Nikolas that I did?'

'How could I tell Nikolas anything?' countered Paige reasonably. 'I expect he knows you better than I ever could.'

'Yes, he does.'

Ariadne sounded smug, but Paige was feeling a little more optimistic. Although she might not be saying anything very much, at least Ariadne was talking to her again. In time, she was sure she could get her to open up to her. She hid a smile. Athens, like Rome, had not been built in a day.

They went down the zigzagging steps to the beach and Paige immediately stepped out of her shoes. She had hoped the girl might follow her example, but she didn't. Instead, she picked her way delicately across to the firmer sand that had been left damp and unblemished by the receding tide.

'So.' Paige determined not to be downhearted. 'You attend school in Athens?'

'Usually.' Ariadne regarded her suspiciously. 'Why do you want to know that?'

'No reason.' Paige sighed. 'I suppose you live with your guardian during term time.'

'With Nikolas, yes.' Ariadne's voice grew soft and dreamy. 'He has a beautiful house near the Plaka. Next year, I will be its mistress.'

For an awful moment, Paige thought she'd said *his* mistress, and her pulse had quickened unsteadily at the thought. 'But surely you'll be going to university next year?' she said, regaining her composure. 'I'm sure—Nikolas—has great plans for your future.'

Ariadne laughed then, the shrill sound jarring on Paige's nerves. 'Nikolas knows what I want,' she said confidently. 'And it is not to go to the university, Miss Tennant.'

Paige didn't push it—but whether that was because she didn't believe what Ariadne was saying or because she did she couldn't say. In any event, it was nothing to do with her, she assured herself. She was only here for the summer...

'Did you go to the university, Miss Tennant?'

Ariadne was asking her a question now, and Paige had to shake herself to remember why she was here. 'Um—no,' she said, after a moment, marshalling her scattered thoughts. 'No, I didn't.' She turned to look at the sea. 'Oh, look! Is that a windsurfer, do you think?'

Ariadne gave the distant sails only a cursory glance. 'It looks like a dinghy,' she said, without interest. 'Why didn't you go to the university, Miss Tennant?'

Paige shrugged, realising she was going to have to give an explanation, even if it did bring back memories she would sooner forget. 'My mother died when I was seventeen,' she said. 'My father took her death rather badly. It didn't seem appropriate to leave him at that time.'

'But he had your sister, did he not?'

'Yes, but she was only a child. He needed someone older. Someone who could—act as his hostess, when he needed one.'

'As I do with Nikolas,' agreed Ariadne triumphantly. ' I am glad you realise that at seventeen I am no longer a child, Miss Tennant. Nikolas forgets it sometimes, I think.' She gave a slow, secretive smile that made Paige feel rather uneasy. 'But only sometimes, *ohi*?'

Paige decided belatedly that she'd asked for that. Ariadne took every opportunity to emphasise the close relationship she had with her guardian. But it was hard enough for Paige to keep her own memories at bay, without encouraging Ariadne to think she'd found a confidante.

'I suppose you have lots of friends of your own age in Athens,' she said positively. 'What do you do in your free time?'

'That depends on what Nikolas is doing,' replied Ariadne at once. 'What do you do, Miss Tennant? Are you sad because there is no man in your life?'

'There are men in my life,' said Paige, determining again not to let the girl irritate her. 'And there are more important things in life than having a boyfriend, Ariadne.' She spread her arms. 'Isn't this a beautiful place? You're so lucky. And what a view. You can see for miles and miles—'

'You do not have to pretend with me, Miss Tennant,' Ariadne declared, and Paige's nerves tightened resignedly. 'I think Nikolas was right. I think you did take this job because your—your *aravoniastikos*—your fiancé—let you down.'

Paige's mouth dropped and her arms fell to her sides. 'What did you say?'

'You were going to be married, were you not?' Ariadne enquired innocently. 'I am sure that is what Nikolas said. But something happened. Your engagement was severed. That is why you were so eager to get away from London. To put some distance between you and this man who hurt you so much.'

Paige was finding it incredibly difficult to breathe normally. 'Nikolas,' she choked, trying not to reveal her anguish. 'Nikolas told you that?'

'But of course.' Ariadne was complacent. 'Nikolas tells me everything, Miss Tennant.' She tilted her head to one side. 'You are upset, but you must forgive him.' Her smile was almost triumphant now. 'He has betrayed your confidence, but do not worry. I will not reveal your unhappiness to anyone else.'

Paige dragged air into her lungs. Was the girl lying? Had Nikolas discussed the circumstances behind her acceptance of the position with his ward? It seemed unlikely. He'd even stopped Ariadne asking her personal questions. Why had he done that if he'd intended to tell her himself?

So how had she found out?

Whatever the truth of the matter, Paige had no intention of feeding the girl's ego. 'Well,' she murmured, with admirable composure, 'he must have misunderstood.'

'What do you mean?'

Ariadne was wary, and Paige knew she mustn't overplay her hand. 'Well, I wasn't sure if he'd believed Martin,' she admitted ruefully. 'But—obviously he did.'

'Martin?' Ariadne looked puzzled now. 'Who is this…this Martin?'

'But I thought you knew,' said Paige, and was half relieved when Ariadne showed she did not. 'Martin is the man I'd agreed to marry. My father introduced us, and for a time I thought it was going to work. But we really had nothing in common. He's really rather immature. It was quite a relief when we broke up.'

Ariadne brooded on this for a few moments, and then she said, 'So what has this Martin to do with your accepting this position?'

'Ah.' Paige realised that if Nikolas had told his ward anything he hadn't been totally indiscreet. 'Well, Martin knows your guardian, and when he heard he was looking for someone to spend the summer here with you on Skiapolis he suggested I should apply for the job.'

Ariadne hunched her shoulders. 'But I thought—'

'It doesn't really matter what you thought.' Paige managed not to show her own frustration. 'If Nikolas chose to tell you he rescued me from a desperate situation, that's only his interpretation of the facts. I'm sorry if you feel I'm ungrateful, but I can't have you thinking some man has broken my heart.'

Well, not that man, anyway, Paige conceded bitterly, still resentful that Nikolas had chosen to share any part of her history with his ward. Martin had let her down, it was true, and she had been hurt by his betrayal. But compared to the pain Nikolas had inflicted it barely counted at all.

Ariadne had to content herself with this explanation. She wasn't happy about it, obviously, but in the absence of any proof to the contrary she had no choice. Paige, meanwhile, was glad to get it out of the way, but she determined to be very careful about what she had to say to Nikolas in future. She'd never dreamed he'd betray her confidence to someone else.

It was almost lunchtime by the time they returned to the

house, and after another alfresco meal Paige was grateful to relax by the pool for a while. Ariadne wasn't exactly a friendly companion, but at least she wasn't sniping at her all the time. In fact, they had quite an interesting discussion about the kind of music they both enjoyed, and Paige decided the girl simply wasn't used to making conversation. She certainly seemed more amenable than before.

But perhaps that was because she didn't consider Paige any competition. Sophie had disappeared into the house after her meal and it was easier when she wasn't making provocative remarks. She emerged some time later, red-faced and sweating from her exertions. She'd found the gym, she explained, and she'd been using the equipment. Anything to work off the handful of calories she'd consumed at lunch, Paige reflected drily.

'They've got everything!' Sophie exclaimed, flinging herself down on the lounger beside her sister. 'There's a step-machine and a treadmill, and all that stuff for strengthening your arms and legs. You ought to try it, Paige. You might enjoy it. You're always saying you'd like to knock a few pounds off your butt.'

Paige couldn't remember ever saying that, and she cast a resigned glance in Ariadne's direction. This was just the sort of ammunition she could use, if she chose to. She was annoyed with her sister for bringing it up.

'Does everything have to come down to weight with you?' she demanded shortly. 'At least I'm not just—just skin and bone!'

'Nor am I.' If there was one thing Sophie didn't like it was being told she was skinny. 'God, you're so touchy! What's the matter? Is Ariadne getting you down?'

'No—'

'Why don't you go and take a shower?' broke in the Greek girl disdainfully. 'It isn't very feminine to—to smell.'

'How would you know?' Sophie rounded on her as the

easier target. 'I doubt if you've ever done anything energetic in your life.'

'You are so—so—'

Ariadne couldn't find the words, and Sophie snorted disparagingly. 'All you ever do is sit around criticising other people,' she said contemptuously. 'When you're not mooning after Petronides, of course.' She put two fingers into her mouth in a deliberate gesture. 'No wonder you've got no friends of your own age. Get a life!'

Paige gave an inward groan. Sophie had just undone all the progress she'd made. It didn't matter that she'd been thinking the same thing earlier. Sophie had no right to make fun of the other girl because she'd noticed she had a crush on Nikolas. As Ariadne's parents were dead, it was natural that all her love and affection were focussed on her guardian.

'Sophie—' she protested, but Ariadne was ahead of her.

'I do not—what was that you said? Moon? Yes, moon about Nikolas,' she cried sharply.

'Sure you do.' Sophie was unrepentant. 'I've seen the way you look at him. If it wasn't so laughable, it'd be pathetic!'

'That's not true.' Ariadne was incensed now, and Paige didn't know how to defuse the situation. 'You don't know anything about my relationship with Nikolas. I am his friend; his confidante. Your sister will tell you that. You could not begin to understand what we share, what we have been through together. You are a child! What would you know about a man like him?'

'About as much as you, I'd say,' replied Sophie scornfully, ignoring Paige's attempt to silence her. 'Get real, Ari. He's not interested in you. For God's sake, he's old enough to be your father. If you're hoping he sees you as anything more than a surrogate daughter, you're going to bomb, big time.'

'You do not know what you are talking about.' Ariadne

was flushed now, her hands moving agitatedly as she spoke. 'I am not a child like you; I am a young woman. I will be eighteen soon, and when I am we will be together. Together, do you understand? He has told me so. He loves me. He is only waiting until I am old enough to announce it to the world. Next year, he is going to make me his wife!'

# CHAPTER NINE

IT WAS a beautiful evening. But then, most evenings were beautiful in the islands, and Paige thought she'd never grow tired of watching the sun sink, bronzed and magnificent, into the horizon.

She smiled at the poetic turn of phrase. There were plenty of young men on Skiapolis who fitted that description, too. Not least, her employer, she conceded drily, though she'd managed to avoid thinking of him for several days. She'd confined her waking hours to doing the job she was being paid for, and despite its shaky beginnings she still believed she was making some progress.

Her bare toes curled into the sand, and the skirt of the voile shift she was wearing blew softly about her legs. It was unusual for her to be on the beach so late, but Ariadne had a headache this evening, and Paige had decided to take a stroll before having dinner in her room.

Sophie was making do with fruit, as usual. She seldom joined her sister and the Greek girl for the evening meal. But there had been no more violent confrontations like that one that had taken place a week ago, and Paige had decided not to play the heavy at night.

There was no doubt it was easier to deal with Ariadne when her sister wasn't there. Despite the uneasy truce that had prevailed since the afternoon after Nikolas's departure, both girls seemed to feel the need to compete with one another whenever they could. Paige was tired of acting as a mediator, and it was so pleasant to have this time to herself.

Still, the week had passed fairly uneventfully on the whole, and although Ariadne could still be a pain sometimes Paige did feel some sympathy for her. It was obvious she was a lonely girl and she evidently adored Nikolas. Which wasn't so surprising. Paige knew to her own cost that he was fatally easy to love.

As far as the things Ariadne had claimed were concerned, Paige was inclined to take them with a pinch of salt. She was fairly sure Nikolas had no idea how the girl felt about him, and the idea that he might be considering marrying his ward was too ludicrous to be true. Or was it? Just occasionally, Paige had felt a twinge of unease. But it was really nothing to do with her, she'd told herself. And there was no doubt that Ariadne would make an ideal wife.

But not for him…

Paige sighed. If only the girl acted more like Sophie. Oh, not rebelliously, she didn't mean that, but more light-heartedly; more her own age. When they'd gone into Agios Petros, as they'd done a couple of times in the past week, Sophie had flirted outrageously with the waiters in the café, where they went for morning coffee, or with the young men who whistled as they walked along the quay. Conversely, Ariadne had remained rigidly indifferent, ignoring any friendly overtures that had come her way.

Which was probably just as well, Paige conceded now, digging her toes into the damp sand as she walked towards the water. She doubted Nikolas would approve if his ward became too friendly with the locals. He might encourage her to make friends, but with the sons or daughters of people he knew, people he socialised with.

Just as her own father had done, when she was younger. Though Parker Tennant had seldom introduced her to *young* men. In the main, the men he'd had dealings with had been older. The younger ones hadn't been influential enough for him.

Was business always conducted that way? she wondered. Did people really attend dinner or cocktail parties without networking the room? Not in her experience, she brooded

ruefully. From the time she'd accompanied her father to
her first reception, she'd been aware of what he'd expected
of her, of the role he'd intended her to play.

By the time she'd met Nikolas, Paige remembered, she'd
already begun to balk at the restrictions her father had
placed on her. Yet, because he'd seemed happier than he'd
done since her mother's death, she'd struggled to hide her
feelings from him.

They'd met at a cocktail party. It was May, and, as well
as the European delegation, Monte Carlo had been busy
with the film festival that was taking place along the coast.
Many famous faces flocked to Monte Carlo to take advantage of the casinos, and Paige had been people-watching
for hours.

She had been feeling particularly good about herself that
evening. She'd spent part of the day sunbathing beside the
hotel pool and her skin had acquired an appealing blush of
peach. The taupe embroidered silk gown she'd worn had
complemented her colouring, and her hair, which in those
days had been quite long, had swung in a soft beige curtain
about her shoulders.

She supposed she had looked different from many of the
women at the reception. She'd worn little make-up for one
thing, and although her clothes were fashionable her father
had always made sure they were not too sophisticated. He'd
wanted her to project an image of youth and innocence,
which he'd known would be especially noticeable in such
surroundings.

Nikolas had arrived at the party with his cousin, Anna.
Paige hadn't known she was his cousin when she was first
introduced. But she'd thought they were two of the most
attractive people she'd ever seen, and she'd envied them
their sophistication.

Of course, her father had encouraged her to talk to them,
and because Nikolas had been so approachable it had been
easier than she'd thought. She'd hardly noticed when her

father had excused himself to speak to someone else. She'd been too bemused, too absurdly flattered, that Nikolas should have wanted to speak to her.

He'd told her that he wasn't staying in Monte Carlo itself. That he had a yacht, the *Athena*, that was anchored out in the bay. She'd learned later that he'd already hosted a couple of glittering gatherings aboard the yacht earlier in the week. It hadn't surprised her that he'd known a lot of famous people—or that her father had been so eager to be accepted into his circle.

The evening had been magical. For the first time, she'd actually enjoyed herself, talking more about her life and her ambitions than she'd ever done before. Nikolas had seemed really interested in her opinions about everything, and it wasn't until much later that she'd suspected he'd been using her just as much as her father had intended to use him.

The following day a huge bouquet of spring flowers had been delivered to their hotel, with a note from Nikolas inviting Paige and her father to have dinner with him that evening on his yacht. Her father had been delighted, congratulating Paige for effecting the opportunity to talk with him in private, but for once Paige had been reluctant to see the invitation in that light.

Still, to begin with, it had seemed as if Parker Tennant had been right. Nikolas hadn't seemed surprised when the topic of their conversation had turned to business matters soon after their arrival. He'd listened to what her father had to say with bland attention, and if Paige had had doubts that he was as interested in her father's business as he'd seemed she'd kept them to herself. The alternative was too incredible, and she'd never believed for one moment that Nikolas might actually be attracted to her.

But then her father had been called back to London.

A fax had arrived one morning informing him that a client he'd been dealing with for many years had died, and there was some controversy about the terms of his will. Sufficiently so to warrant Parker Tennant's involvement in the distribution of his assets, and Paige had prepared herself for the disappointment of never seeing Nikolas again.

She'd told herself it was for the best. Whatever his intentions were, she'd begun to like him too much, and common sense had warned her that she was courting disaster. A man like Petronides was unlikely to get seriously involved with someone like her. She was too young for him, for one thing, and she shouldn't mistake his kindness for anything else.

But it hadn't turned out as she'd expected.

When her father had phoned the yacht to explain that he was having to cut his visit short, Nikolas had suggested that Paige might like to stay on and spend a few days cruising the Mediterranean. 'Anna will be with us, of course,' he'd added, though Paige had known his assurances were unnecessary. From the moment he'd made the offer, there'd been no question that her father would allow her to refuse.

And so, later that same day, Paige had found herself installed in a luxurious stateroom aboard the *Athena*. As Nikolas had promised, Anna did accompany them—but so did Anna's fiancé, Lukos Panagia—a fact that Nikolas had conveniently forgotten to tell the older man.

Paige shivered now. She remembered that first evening very well. How could she not, when it had been the start of something so momentous in her life? With a warm breeze stirring the smooth surface of the water and the lights of the principality disappearing into the distance, it had seemed like a dream—or perhaps the beginnings of a nightmare, she acknowledged. Whatever, she'd been incredibly excited, and determined to enjoy herself no matter what.

When she'd arrived on deck, she'd discovered that a table had been set beneath an awning. Four places had been laid, but only Nikolas had been standing against the rail, drinking from a tumbler that she had guessed contained whisky. His powerful legs had been braced against the movement of the vessel, his collarless shirt and black mole-skin trousers less formal than she'd been used to...

He turned at her approach, his eyes darkening at the sight of her hovering at the top of the steps that led up from the lower deck. 'You look nervous,' he remarked, viewing her black strappy top and loose chiffon trousers with narrow-eyed intensity. 'Would you rather have returned to London with your father?'

Paige took a breath. 'No,' she admitted honestly. 'I'm—very grateful you invited me to spend a few days on the yacht.'

'Are you?' Nikolas's eyes sparked with sudden impatience. 'Well, perhaps I don't want your gratitude,' he said flatly. 'I invited you to stay because I want us to get to know one another better.' He grimaced. 'Without your father running interference.'

Paige felt a catch in her throat. 'I'm sure you don't mean that,' she murmured, half turning to rest a hand on the rail. 'It's a beautiful evening, isn't it?' Then, forcing a casual tone, she asked, 'Where are Anna and Lukos?'

He didn't answer her. Not immediately anyway. 'Why don't you think I mean it when I say I want to get to know you?' he asked instead, and she shifted from one sandal-clad foot to the other.

'You—you don't have to pretend, Mr Petronides,' she told him steadily, unable to use his given name. While her father was there she'd got away without using either of the alternatives, and he scowled now at her deliberate formality.

'I am not pretending, Paige,' he assured her, with studied patience. 'And I would prefer it if you use my Christian name when you speak to me.' He paused. 'Why should you assume I didn't want you here?'

'I didn't say that, precisely.' Paige chose her words with care. 'I suppose it could have been awkward for you with your cousin *and* her fiancé on board.'

'You think I invited you to join me to—how is it you say it?—to even the score?'

'The numbers,' murmured Paige automatically. 'To even the numbers.' She licked her dry lips. 'I'm sure you understand what I mean. But anyway, I do appreciate it.'

'You know nothing about it.' Nikolas left the rail and crossed the deck towards her. 'You really think I'd do that to you? Make you a—a convenience, *ne*?' He stopped beside her, dark and disturbing in the lights that hung between the bulkhead and the bridge. 'I am not your father, Paige.'

She stiffened. 'What is that supposed to mean?'

But she knew; she knew what he was implying. And, although she was indignant, she couldn't altogether blame him for his interpretation of events.

Nevertheless, she was startled when he put out his hand and stroked the soft curtain of her hair. 'I am sorry,' he said. 'I do not wish for us to be—*ti*—at odds. *Na pari i oryi*, Paige, let us not talk about your father. Please believe me when I say I invited you because I want to spend some time—alone—with you.'

Paige was stunned. 'But Anna and Lukos—'

'—Are here to chaperon you,' declared Nikolas, stroking her hair again. 'Do you think your father would have allowed you to stay on the yacht if—?' He broke off then and when he spoke again he was rueful. 'Well, perhaps he would,' he conceded drily. 'But I would not.'

'You're doing it again.' Paige stepped away from him, her back coming up against the rail. 'I'm sure you told my father that your cousin would be accompanying us.' Her face burned suddenly. 'He's—he's not my—pimp, you know.'

'Now why would you make such a declaration?' Nikolas's mouth twisted sensually, and although he wasn't

touching her Paige could feel his heat penetrating the thin
fabric of her clothes. 'You do know what your father is
like, do you not, *aghapita*? Perhaps you have had some
reason to suspect that what I say is true.'

Paige caught her breath. 'How dare you?'

'How dare I what?' To her dismay, Nikolas had moved
towards her and now she had nowhere to go. 'Paige, I don't
care what his motives were. I don't care if you've done this
before. I'm grateful that you're here now. With me.'

Paige stared up at him, aghast. 'You think I make a habit
of this?'

'Of what, *aghapita*?' He placed one hand on the rail at
either side of her, successfully trapping her within his arms.

'Of—of appearing to be left alone? Of needing someone's protection?' She gazed up at him with horrified eyes.
'Do you think my father arranged the whole thing?'

'If he did, I'm grateful for it.' His eyes on her mouth
were an almost palpable caress. 'Relax, Paige. I won't hurt
you. I am enchanted by your sweetness and your joy of
life.'

Paige shook her head. 'But not by my innocence?' she
said bitterly, and he lifted a hand to cup her hot cheek.

'That, too,' he said, hearing the tremor in her voice as
she accused him. 'Sweet Paige. Do you have any idea how
adorable you are?'

Paige jerked back. 'You're making fun of me.'

'No, I'm not.' His expression sobered, and his hand slid
down to caress her neck. He studied her face with a searching gaze and then added softly, 'If you continue to look at
me with such soulful eyes, I shall begin to think I frighten
you.'

'You don't frighten me.'

But he did, and he knew it. Or rather he knew she was
afraid of the emotions he aroused inside. She wanted to
remain wary of him, to distrust him because of the things

he'd said about her father. But the truth was, he excited her in a way she'd never experienced before.

'So…' His thumb moved sensuously against the fine bones that defined her throat. 'Will you forgive me for what I said?'

Paige could feel her pulse pounding in her ears. 'Do I have a choice?' she asked, finding it difficult to breathe.

'We all have a choice,' replied Nikolas softly. 'You do wish to stay with me, do you not?'

*To stay with him!*

The connotations behind that simple statement were breathtaking. He hadn't asked if she wanted to stay on the yacht; he'd asked her if she wanted to stay with *him*.

'And—and if I don't?' she said, and caught her breath when he bent his head and his tongue brushed her ear.

'Then I should have no choice but to obey your wishes,' he whispered softly. 'But I'm hoping that won't happen.'

Paige's hands came up against his chest. 'You—you had no right to accuse my father of double dealing.'

'I know.'

'He really did get a fax, you know. He didn't want to go back to London and leave me here.'

'I believe you.'

Paige blew out a breath. 'Then why did you say what you did? Why did you let me think you were suspicious of him?' She sighed. 'If Daddy really knew how you felt, he'd never have let me accept your invitation.'

'Wouldn't he?' Once again, there was that note of disbelief in his voice, but before she could remark upon it he spoke again. 'Well…my opinion of your father isn't of any importance,' he declared, tracing a line with his finger from her shoulder to her elbow and beyond. 'I'm far more interested in what you think of me.'

'What I think— Please don't do that.' Paige wrapped her arms about her waist now. 'I'm not a fool, Mr Petronides. You don't have to humour me.' But then, because whatever she said she knew her father wouldn't be very pleased if she offended him, she told him, 'Until this evening, I'd always thought you were a—a very pleasant man.'

'A very pleasant man?' he echoed. '*Theus*, I think that is what you call being damned with faint praise, *ohi*?' His eyes caressed her face and she prayed he couldn't see what she was really thinking. '*Kala*, I do not feel very pleasant at this moment. You have made me feel very cynical and very old.'

'You're not old.'

She said the words automatically, and his eyes narrowed as they focussed on her mouth. 'I'm thirty-five,' he said. 'Almost twice your age. And regrettably far more experienced in the ways of the world.'

Paige moved her shoulders in a nervous gesture. 'More jaded, you mean?' she said, hoping she sounded more confident than she felt. She had the feeling this conversation was becoming far too dangerous for someone of her limited experience and she didn't honestly know where it was going. 'Appearances can be deceptive, you know.'

'Oh, I know.' Nikolas regarded her humorously. 'Who would have thought that such a timid little cat would have such sharp claws?'

Paige looked warily up at him. 'You're making fun of me.'

'Only a little.' He smiled. 'You're so delightful, it's hard to resist.' His hand shaped her cheek. 'Perhaps if you remembered to call me Nikolas I'd stop teasing you. I can't make love to a woman who insists on addressing me as Mr Petronides.'

Paige's jaw dropped. She had no idea what to say. She supposed someone like Anna would have a ready response, but she didn't. The very idea of making love with him was too incredible to consider, and the thought that he might be making fun of her again caused her to turn abruptly towards the rail.

'I—' She sought wildly for some neutral topic and when her eyes discovered lights on the horizon she said stupidly, 'Is—is that a ship?'

'As we are at sea and there are no doubt many ships in our vicinity, it seems likely,' Nikolas remarked, behind her. He moved in closer and once again she was trapped within the circle of his arms. 'Do not be afraid of me, Paige,' he added, his shower-damp hair brushing her cheek as his teeth nibbled her shoulder. 'I promise I will do nothing to hurt you. But I want you and I think that, despite your fears, you want me.'

*He wanted her!*

Paige's knees turned to water, and she was glad she was gripping the rail for support. Not teasing now, she could feel the muscles of his pelvis close behind her and the real-isation that he was becoming aroused caused the blood to thunder in her ears.

When she said nothing, he caught the skin of her neck between his teeth and sucked, very gently. 'You do under-stand what I am saying, don't you, Paige?' he asked hus-kily. 'You knew how I felt about you before you accepted my invitation.'

She hadn't, but to admit it would sound immature and naïve. Instead, she simply lifted one shoulder, as if in silent acknowledgement, and his mouth slid the strap of her satin vest aside and again nuzzled her flesh.

She had to say something then to still the panicky feel-ings inside her. 'Will—will Anna and Lukos be joining us?' she murmured, when she was sure she could speak the words without betraying how she felt. At least he couldn't see her face in the shadows cast by the awning. Here, against the rail, they had a small measure of privacy from the rest of the ship.

'Not yet.' Nikolas's voice had harshened slightly, she noticed. 'Not until much later,' he added, taking a deep breath. 'Forget about my cousin and her fiancé. I imagine they have better things to do than to think about us.'

*Oh, God!*

Paige realised then that he really did think she was used to this. When his hand caressed her waist and then shifted upwards so that his thumb was brushing the underside of her breast, she had to stifle the moan that rose into her throat. Yet, despite her inexperience, she knew he was right: that she wanted to give in to him. However ignorant of sex she was, she had no trouble in understanding her own body's needs.

He turned her then, both hands at her midriff now, reminding her of how alone she was. And he knew all the moves; all the ways to make her want him. And, dangerous as it was, she couldn't stop herself from looking up into his dark face.

He was so attractive. Her pulse quickened uncontrollably as his dark gaze moved over her upturned face. Her lips parted, unknowingly provocative, inviting his tongue's invasion. Her breasts puckered delicately, tightening the satin across their swollen peaks.

He bent towards her, his lips seeking hers, feathering light butterfly kisses across her mouth. He was in no hurry, whereas Paige was eager for him to kiss her properly, the hunger he was arousing in her making her a stranger to herself.

Her hands came up without her volition, gripping his neck and bringing his mouth to hers. 'Tell me what you want,' he urged, when he heard the frantic sounds she was making, but Paige could only press herself closer, her breasts cushioned by the muscled hardness of his chest.

He groaned then, his hands sliding down her back to bring her fully against him, and his kiss grew more urgent, his tongue sliding hungrily into her mouth. Paige had thought she would be frightened of the power he had over her, but the need he was creating inside her demanded to be met.

Her senses swam. A kind of mindless delight had taken over her body, making any kind of resistance futile. She was suddenly so close to him that she could feel every bone and sinew, and the throbbing heat of his erection pressed hard against her stomach.

Excitement pulsed along her veins, making her nerves tingle, turning her blood to fire. His hands slid beneath the hem of the satin top and discovered she was not wearing a bra and she trembled with anticipation. No man had ever been this intimate with her before and the fears she'd had earlier fled before the sensual pleasure of his touch.

He murmured to her in his own language, telling her she was beautiful, urging her to believe him when he said he'd wanted her from the moment he'd first seen her. When he lowered his head to suckle her nipples, she realised he'd exposed her breasts to his possessive gaze. At once, an unfamiliar slickness was palpable between her legs, a pool of heat that dampened the bikini briefs she was wearing.

'Come,' he said at last. Taking her hand, he drew her across the deck and down a short companionway to his stateroom. 'Much as I would like to make love to you on deck, we cannot scandalise Captain Stavros. Besides,' he added huskily, 'I want to look at you. I want to see your face when I finally make you mine.'

Paige reflected now that he had given her an opportunity to stop him. She hadn't been unaware of what she was doing when she'd accompanied him to his cabin. She hadn't even had the excuse of having drunk too much and he had taken advantage of her. In fact, in many ways, she had taken advantage of him.

She sighed. She supposed she'd been carried away by her first real experience of sexual passion. Men had kissed her before; some of them had even wanted to make love to her. But none of them had affected her as Nikolas had done. Neither before nor since, she added painfully. She'd been lucky nothing more had come of it. Thankfully, it had been the wrong time of the month for her to conceive.

Of course, Nikolas had had no idea how inexperienced she was. She must have been a better actress than she'd thought, she mused, half amazed at the self-possession she'd shown when he'd undressed her. Perhaps it had been the subtle ambience of the cabin: the stateroom had been lamplit and romantic, bronzed shades casting a golden light over the dais where the bed was set. Silk sheets, cool against her back; the fragrance of soap and shaving lotions; and the musky scent of Nikolas's body as it crushed hers to the mattress.

Whatever, she'd been too bemused to do anything but watch the master at work. Her only moment of trepidation had been when she'd seen the rearing power of his arousal, but when he'd drawn her hand to him she'd touched him eagerly, revelling in the pulsing life she could feel within the clasp of her fingers.

The need that throbbed in his loins had seduced her. With a sensuality she hadn't known she possessed until that night, she'd surrendered eagerly to his demands. Everything he'd done, every breath he'd taken from her, every scorching touch that had drawn her even further into his sensuous web, had been given freely, and she'd ached for the knowledge she knew only he could impart.

But Nikolas had been in no hurry, she remembered. Despite his own obvious needs, he'd indulged himself in a long and languid exploration of her body first. He'd even kissed each one of her toes before tracing a line of kisses up her calf to the sensitive hollow at the back of her knee. Then on to the quivering flesh of her inner thigh.

By the time he'd buried his face in the moist curls at the junction of her legs and tasted her with his tongue, Paige had been unable to stop shaking. Nikolas had been trembling, too, she recalled, the control he'd been exerting up until then slowly slipping away. It was probably that evidence of his own vulnerability that had robbed her of any inhibitions, she thought tremulously. Looking back now, she had to admire the courage she'd shown in not betraying how innocent she was.

Nikolas had soon found out, however. But by then it had been much too late for him to do anything about it. She'd shown such passion, such unknowing skill, he'd been totally convinced of her experience, but she hadn't been able to stifle her cry of pain when he'd thrust into muscles that had never known a man's invasion before.

The memory could still disturb her, she discovered. Had she really been so naïve as to believe that Nikolas wanted anything more from her than sex? She acknowledged now that it had been the only time in her life when she'd truly trusted a man. Since then, she'd had good reason to regret her gullibility.

Yet, at the time, she'd had no reason to doubt him. In fact, Nikolas had been tenderly solicitous of her needs. Although his lovemaking couldn't have turned out as he'd expected, the only anger he'd shown had been towards himself.

He had made love to her again. But only because she'd begged him to do it. Perhaps, also, he'd wanted to leave her with a happier memory than the pain his first attempt had achieved. Whatever the reason, that second time had been magical. She remembered she'd steeled herself for it, dreading the moment when the sensitive muscles would rebel. But instead there'd been no pain, only an expanding sensitivity, and ultimately a satisfaction so intense, she'd cried for the beauty of their love…

# CHAPTER TEN

THE realisation that waves were curling about her ankles now brought Paige to her senses. She'd been so wrapped up in her thoughts, she hadn't noticed the rising tide, and she sighed in frustration when she saw the stains of sea-water on the hem of her dress. It flapped against her legs, cooling her emotions, reminding her of where she was and why she'd been so absorbed.

No wonder she'd been so unsure about coming here, she thought ruefully. Seeing Nikolas again had stirred up more than just memories of the past. But if she wanted to keep this job she had to put their previous relationship behind her. She was only tormenting herself by remembering how sweet it had been.

Sweet, but brief, she sighed regretfully. The day after he'd made love to her in his cabin, Nikolas had begged her forgiveness for taking advantage of her, and insisted it would never happen again. Despite her unwillingness to forget it, he'd spent the remainder of the cruise trying to make it up to her, and her confusion had been expunged by the tenderness he'd shown towards her.

Paige remembered she'd thought it was because he really cared about her. She wouldn't have believed he could treat her with such care and consideration unless he'd had some genuine feelings for her. As for herself, she'd fallen madly in love with him, and she was sure both Anna and Lukos thought Nikolas felt the same.

When her father had returned, unexpectedly, some five days later, she couldn't wait to tell him how she felt. Nikolas had had a call from Parker Tennant asking him if he could arrange to put his daughter ashore at some point convenient to them both. Nikolas's answer had been to propose that her father meet the yacht at Piraeus. He had gone on to suggest that Tennant might like to come aboard and sail with them to Skiapolis. He'd issued an invitation to them both to spend a few days at his villa there, and Paige had been thrilled at what she'd seen as this evidence of his intent.

From the moment her father had come on board the *Athena* however, she'd known that something was wrong. He'd confessed to having a headache, but, although he'd tried to hide it, it had been obvious to her that it was more than that. She'd also noticed that when Nikolas wasn't looking the glances her father had cast in his direction had been strangely malevolent. She'd hardly been able to contain herself until she could speak to him alone.

But, in the event, it had been the following afternoon before she'd had a chance to share his confidence. Although it had still been light when they'd arrived at the small harbour of Agios Petros, her father was clearly not well. He'd been subject to migraines for years, and he'd been obliged to retire to his suite of rooms immediately. In consequence, Paige had spent a rather anxious evening wondering what was going on.

The following day, she and Nikolas—and Yanis, who had been staying on the island in his employer's absence— had spent the morning touring the island. Her father had been invited to join them, but although he'd been looking much better Parker Tennant had decided to stay at the house. A wise precaution, Nikolas had said, but Paige had had her own ideas about why her father hadn't come. She'd consoled herself with the thought that if he'd had any reason not to trust Nikolas he wouldn't have encouraged her to go with him. And as it was it had been difficult not to enjoy herself with the two men when Nikolas had made it so obvious that he considered her special.

After lunch, Nikolas and his assistant had excused themselves to attend to business. Several matters, which had arisen while Nikolas was away, had required his attention, and Paige and her father had sought a sheltered spot beside the pool. Paige had been relieved to see that some of the tension had left her father's face and he was actually looking quite cheerful. He'd even smiled when she'd curled up on the lounger beside him.

She should have been warned, she supposed now. Whenever her father had smiled at her like that, it had usually meant she was doing something he wanted. Since his death, she'd been forced to accept that Parker Tennant had seldom considered her feelings at all.

He'd begun by telling her how pleased he was that she and Nikolas were getting along together so well. He'd confessed that their host had told him what a pleasure it had been to entertain his daughter, and that he was obviously interested in her. Which was just as well, he'd added, confusing her a little, because he'd had no success in getting him to invest in the Murchison deal.

He was depending on her to persuade him, he'd said confidently, accompanying this assertion with a conspiratorial smile. It was obvious Nikolas would do anything for her if she asked him to, he'd insisted, and if he did prove reluctant she should sweeten the request in any way he chose.

Paige had been appalled. The idea that her father should virtually suggest that she go to bed with Nikolas to gain some kind of advantage over him had horrified her. Too late she'd remembered the comments Nikolas had made about her father and her reaction to them. Suddenly, they'd seemed all too valid, and even Nikolas's seduction had been tainted by the suspicion that he'd known what her father had intended all along.

At first, she'd pretended not to understand him. She'd tried to be sympathetic, even though her heart had been heavy with dread. But there'd been no mistake: her father expected her to use any influence she had to gain what he wanted. And when, albeit reluctantly, she'd confessed what had happened, he'd called her a fool and a traitor, which had destroyed any lingering doubts she might have had.

The horror of that day still had the strength to depress her. What she had treasured as a gift had turned into a burden. She'd had nowhere to turn. No one she could turn to. She'd only known she had to get away without seeing Nikolas again.

That was when Yanis had come to her rescue. He'd found her in a corner of the garden, desperately trying to come to terms with what she'd learned. He hadn't asked any questions, but, seeing her ravaged face, he'd probably assumed Nikolas was to blame. In any event, he'd arranged for a boat to take her to the nearby island of Mykonos, and from there she'd been able to get a flight back to England.

Her father had come after her. He'd obviously realised how abominably he'd behaved, and he'd spent the rest of that summer trying to make it up to her. He'd blamed Nikolas for his behaviour, of course, accusing the other man of stringing him along with empty promises, of only using him as a way to get to her. He'd never had any intention of investing with Tennants, Parker had insisted, and when weeks passed and Nikolas hadn't even tried to contact her Paige had come to the painful conclusion that her father had been right all along.

Her only consolation had been the fact that she hadn't waited for Nikolas to ask her to leave. She was sure that that must have annoyed him a lot. He wasn't used to women using him, and her walking out as she had must have irritated him enormously. Perhaps that was why he'd jumped at the chance to get his own back by making her his employee.

If so, it would explain why he'd been so angry that morning when he'd kissed her. Despite himself, there must still remain some shred of sexual attraction towards her, after

all. Not that it was of any advantage to her, feeling as she
did about him. Until she'd seen him again, she hadn't realised how deep and vulnerable her wounds still were.

But she didn't want to think about that now. Treading
into deeper water, which was now threaded with moonlight,
she allowed the waves to surge about her thighs. Her dress
was ruined anyway. Salt water did terrible things to fine
fabrics. And besides, there was a certain appeal to destroying something beautiful in her present mood.

Was that how Nikolas had felt when he'd seduced her?
Had he enjoyed thwarting a man for whom he'd obviously
had no respect? What had he thought when he'd discovered
her innocence? she wondered. Had he felt any remorse for
what he'd done? Or had he considered that her father's
behaviour had warranted no remission? That the victory
had been sweeter than he could have hoped?

Her body was hot now and over-stimulated by the unwilling feelings she had instigated, and, choking back a sob,
she waded further into the sea. Her dress was soaked, clinging sensuously to her body, and when she looked down she
saw her nipples outlined in sharp relief.

The sight was absurdly provocative somehow, and, although her hands went to pull the cloth away, when her
fingers touched her breasts they didn't obey her commands.
Memories of the way Nikolas had caressed them had created an overwhelming need inside her, and she touched
them almost reverently, afraid of the dark emotions spiral-
ling in her head.

Oh, God, she thought, horror overtaking her, and she
raised her arms above her head in an agony of self-disgust.
Was this what she was reduced to? Living a life in her
imagination? How amused Nikolas would be if he could
see her now.

'*Perimeno!* Paige! In God's name, come back!'

The hoarse cry that arrested her came from the shore.
Turning, all she could see was a dark figure waving at her,

and for a heart-stopping moment she thought it was her
father's ghost. But Parker Tennant had never been so tall
or so broad, nor moved with such arrogance. As he
splashed into the shallows and the moonlight fell on his
dark face, she saw it was the man she least wanted to see.

She trembled then, and for the first time she realised how
cold the water was. Or perhaps it was the fact that her dress
was wet and clinging clammily to her. Whatever the reason,
she had no choice but to turn back.

'Go back,' she cried, when he came further into the water, and, tucking her tumbled hair behind her ears, she
started towards the shore. What was he doing here? she
wondered. Kiria Papandreiu had said he wasn't expected
back for another three days. She'd never have taken such
liberties if she'd had any suspicion that he might find her.

He didn't do as she asked. When she came within reach,
he grabbed her wrist and tugged her ruthlessly back onto
the beach. 'Are you mad?' he demanded, when she was
standing, shivering, in front of him. 'What were you trying
to do? Kill yourself?'

Paige drew a steadying breath. 'Of course not.'

'Of course not?' He mimicked her denial with harsh disbelief. 'Paige, I saw you. You were about to dive into the
water. No one goes swimming fully clothed.'

'I wasn't going swimming,' protested Paige, wishing
she'd brought a towel with her. 'I—I was paddling, and I
got out of my depth.'

Nikolas scowled, his dark face with its unfamiliar
shadow of beard strangely tense. 'Paddling,' he muttered
incredulously. 'Paige, this is me you're talking to. No one
goes paddling at this time of the evening. Besides, you're
not the type.'

Paige held up her head. 'So what type am I?'

Nikolas shook his head. 'That's not the point.'

'What is the point, then?' she asked. 'And why should
you think you have the right to tell me what to do? If I

want to go swimming after dark, that's my business, not yours.'

'Not so long as you are here,' he retorted frustratedly. He noticed she was shivering, and, stripping off his suit jacket, he swung it about her shoulders without another word. 'As long as you are living on Skiapolis, you are my responsibility. For pity's sake, Paige, tell me this was a mistake.'

She wanted to shrug his jacket off. There would have been some satisfaction in having it fall on the sand at her feet. But it was warm and comforting and it smelled of him, of the heated strength of his body. It reminded her of where it had been until a few seconds ago.

'I'm wet,' she said instead, and his expression softened.

'I know,' he said, looking down at her, and she was intensely conscious that she was no longer feeling so cold.

'Your jacket will be ruined,' she murmured, trying to instil some shred of practicality into the moment, and his dark lashes dipped to shade his glittering eyes.

'Do you think I care?' he demanded, and she knew he was aware of the sudden intimacy that had flowered between them. '*Theus*, Paige, I was at the top of the cliff when I saw you. I've never come down those steps so fast.'

'But—you could have fallen,' she protested, almost anxiously, and his lips twisted at her sudden concern.

'Yes, I could,' he agreed. 'Does it matter?'

'Of course it matters. You could have been killed!'

Paige was frustrated by his indifference, but she broke off abruptly when Nikolas's hand trailed softly across her throat. 'Would you have cared?' he asked. 'Or would you have said I deserved it? Perhaps it would give you some pleasure to be chief mourner at my funeral.'

'Don't joke about such things.' Paige dashed his hand away and struggled to take a steadying breath. 'In any case, what are you doing here? I thought you weren't supposed to be back until the end of the week.'

'I changed my mind.'

Nikolas loosened his tie and pulled it free of his collar, and she realised he must have come straight down to the beach before doing anything else. He was still wearing the suit in which he'd flown from Athens. She hadn't heard the helicopter, but as it flew in over the other side of the island that wasn't so surprising. Besides, her ears had been filled with the thunderous roar of the sea.

'It was as well I did,' he added now, and the shadows couldn't hide the impatience that still showed in his face. 'If I'd not been here—'

'I'd have had to do without this gallant gesture?' Paige interrupted him, and despite her reluctance to remove it she swung his jacket from her shoulders and thrust it back into his hands. 'I'm sorry it's so wet, but I did warn you.'

Nikolas scowled. 'Keep it,' he said shortly. 'I don't need it.'

'Nor do I,' lied Paige, deciding this conversation had gone on long enough. She began to edge round him, saying politely, 'I'm grateful for your concern, but I'm perfectly capable of looking after myself.'

'Are you?' Nikolas swore then. 'But you haven't forgiven me, have you? You haven't forgotten what I said before I went away.'

Paige stiffened. 'Before you went away?' She shook her head. 'Oh, you mean when you accused me of provoking you?' she declared, with what she thought was admirable inconsequence. She held up her head. 'Well, I haven't been fretting about it, if that's what you think.'

She had paused to deliver this denunciation, but she realised her mistake when his fingers circled the chilled skin of her upper arm. The memory of what she'd been thinking about before he'd interrupted her was still too vivid, and she felt appalled and excited, all at the same time.

'I shouldn't have said what I did,' he muttered, his thumb moving almost abrasively against her damp flesh. '*Theus,*

Paige, sometimes I think you are intent on destroying my peace of mind.'

'Your peace of mind?' Somehow she got the words past her frozen lips. 'So this is all to do with you, not me.' She looked pointedly at his restraining fingers. 'I think you should let me go.'

'I think so, too.'

But he didn't do it. Instead, Paige felt the warmth spreading from his hand along the whole length of her arm. His eyes drifted over her, causing an almost palpable heat to invade her breasts, to surge into her throat and fill her face with fiery colour.

Which, thankfully, he couldn't see. But that didn't stop her from tingling all over in anticipation of his touch. Or prevent the needs he was arousing and the pulse deep inside that demanded to be stilled.

But she couldn't allow that to happen.

With a feeling of desperation, she knew she had to stop this before she totally lost her mind. She was allowing emotions, feelings she should have more sense than to nurture, to blind her to the realities of the situation. She didn't know what he was thinking, what unwilling impulse was driving him on. She only knew what he chose to tell her, and did she really want the humiliation of being at his mercy again?

'Let me go, Nikolas,' she said, without any real hope of his obeying her. And then she realised she had the perfect way to achieve her ends. 'It would be difficult to justify your behaviour to Ariadne,' she added, her confidence hardening at the memory. She was so stupid. She'd almost forgotten what the younger girl had said.

'To Ariadne?' Nikolas had bent his head to bestow a lingering kiss on her bare shoulder, but now he lifted his head and looked at her with narrowing eyes. 'Why would I feel the need to justify what I do to her?'

'Well, you tell her everything, don't you?' Paige taunted, gaining strength from his obvious confusion. 'You even told her why I took this position. Why I was foolish enough to believe every word you said.'

'I think not—'

'Oh, I think so.' Paige was determined not to let him get the upper hand. 'How was it Ariadne put it? Oh, yes. She said that you'd told her you'd only offered me the job because you felt sorry for me.'

*'Iseh trelos!'*

Nikolas spoke harshly and, although she didn't understand his words, she understood his anger very well. 'You can't deny it. She told me everything,' she insisted steadily. 'Apparently, I was desperate to put some distance between me and the man who had—who had let me down.'

*'Then ineh alithia!* That's not true!' Nikolas exclaimed furiously, and Paige despised herself for the sense of loss she felt when his hand fell away from her arm.

'But it is true, isn't it?' Paige demanded painfully. 'To all intents and purposes, she wasn't telling a lie.'

'She did not get any information from me,' said Nikolas grimly. 'In God's name, Paige, what do you think I am?'

Paige shook her head. 'So—are you calling her a liar?'

'I—no.' He raked back his hair with an impatient hand. 'You must have misunderstood.'

'What was there to misunderstand?' countered Paige coldly, all warmth draining out of her. She took a deep breath. 'I suppose you thought Ariadne was too polite to betray your confidence, but you were wrong. It gave her a great deal of pleasure to humiliate me.'

'You're exaggerating.'

'Am I?' Paige gave him a pitying look before starting towards the cliff. 'Well, once again we'll have to agree to disagree, won't we? And now, if you'll excuse me, I would like to get out of these wet clothes.'

# CHAPTER ELEVEN

PAIGE half expected to wake up the next morning with a chill or a streaming cold at least. Indeed, she'd half hoped she would. Anything to give her an excuse to avoid seeing Nikolas again in the immediate future. But either the warmth of the evening air had protected her, or she was hardier than she'd thought, because she found she had no unpleasant symptoms at all.

Not unless you could call an uneasy feeling in the pit of your stomach an unpleasant symptom, she thought ruefully. And a tendency for her palms to become uncomfortably damp. But there was no doubt that, psychologically, she was suffering. Much more than any outward signs could betray.

However, in the event, she needn't have worried. It appeared that Nikolas was as reluctant to spend any time with her as she was with him. Apart from occasional glimpses of him walking in the gardens with Yanis, or crossing the hall of the villa, he spent most of his time closeted in his study, taking all his meals with his assistant and no one else.

Paige assumed he spent some time with Ariadne. The girl was occasionally absent for no apparent reason and when she returned from wherever she'd been she looked as smug as a bee in clover. If Nikolas had chided her for her indiscretion, she'd got over it, and on the whole the household functioned much as it had while its master was away.

For her part, she was persevering with her relationship with Ariadne. Although there was still something about the girl she didn't like, there was no doubt that they'd achieved a level of communication that made Paige's job easier.

Ariadne was still unwilling to spend time on the beach, but she did now, occasionally, join Paige and her sister in the pool. And, before her guardian had returned, Paige had encouraged her to play tennis in the mornings. Ariadne didn't put much effort into her game, but that, combined with a minor programme of aerobics that Paige had devised, had helped to put some much needed colour into her face.

All in all, Paige considered she was being reasonably successful at her task, and were it not for Nikolas's presence and her continuing awareness of it she believed she'd be moderately content. Sophie seemed happy, which in itself was a minor miracle. She was away from the undesirable influences she had had in London, and although she was still avoiding dinner most evenings she didn't appear to be losing any weight.

And then one evening, about a week after Nikolas's return to Skiapolis, Paige discovered her sister's secret.

Despite her reluctance to run into Nikolas, Paige had continued to dine downstairs. She and Ariadne—and occasionally Yanis—often shared a table on the patio, and, although there were obviously pitfalls to avoid, generally speaking they were quite pleasant occasions. To begin with, Ariadne had been stand-offish with Yanis, and Paige guessed she considered that dining with an employee was hardly the done thing. But Paige had pointed out that she was an employee, too, and Yanis deserved just as much respect as anyone else.

Whether Ariadne had accepted that was questionable. But as he worked with her guardian and was obviously in his confidence she'd evidently decided not to rock the boat. Besides, Yanis was fun. He had a wealth of stories compiled during the almost thirty years he'd worked for the Petronides family. Paige always found it fascinating listening to him reminisce about Nikolas's father and grandfather, the latter having founded the shipping line that Nikolas now controlled.

In consequence, she rarely went up to her room before ten o'clock. And, because Sophie usually retired so much earlier, she'd never disturbed her sister when she went up to bed. Sometimes, she'd wished Sophie was awake, so that she could share some particular anecdote with her. But she'd always decided it would wait until the next day. They had plenty of time to talk during the long afternoons when Ariadne went to rest.

On the evening she found out what Sophie was doing, Paige had had dinner alone. Neither Yanis nor Ariadne had joined her at the table on the patio, and she'd assumed they were having dinner together. It was possible they'd gone out, of course. She knew from past experience that Nikolas had friends on the island. Nevertheless, she didn't enjoy eating alone, and as it was only a quarter to nine when she went upstairs she decided to see if Sophie was still awake.

She wouldn't admit it, but she was desperate for company. Despite her determination not to let Nikolas's attitude bother her, this past week had been something of a strain on her nerves. It was all right when she was busy or when there was someone else around to distract her. But she wasn't sleeping particularly well and she had no desire to spend the rest of the evening alone in her room.

She knocked at Sophie's door, and when there was no response she opened it. She'd guessed her sister was sitting on the balcony and hadn't heard her. But when she switched on a lamp she found the room was empty. The balcony, too, was deserted. Wherever Sophie was it wasn't here.

Refusing to allow herself to panic, Paige went out of the room again and looked up and down the shadowy corridor. The lamps were lit, and their illumination glinted softly on sculptured alcoves and jewel-toned vases, elegant paintings and long draperies that moved in the air-conditioned draught. But there was no sight or sound of her sister. The corridor was deserted. She could almost believe she was alone in the house.

Taking a steadying breath, she closed Sophie's door again and went back to her own room. Then, twisting her hands together, she paced anxiously across the floor. She had to think, she thought. There was a logical explanation for this, if she could think of it. Could it possibly have anything to do with the fact that she'd had dinner alone?

But that was clutching at straws, and she knew it. She couldn't believe that Sophie and Ariadne were likely to have gone out together. Yet it was possible, she supposed, and the fact that Yanis hadn't joined her tonight probably meant that he had dined with Nikolas. But surely Sophie would have told her if she and Ariadne had planned to spend the evening elsewhere?

She shook her head. No. She had to think of another explanation. Sophie must be in the house somewhere. She couldn't be anywhere else. Unless she'd gone for a walk. After all, it was what she herself had done on another occasion. But she didn't want to think about that now. Or about the fact that Sophie wasn't likely to walk alone.

Paige's mouth went dry as an alternative explanation occurred to her. What if Sophie made a habit of going out in the evening? What if that was why she never joined them for dinner? What if somewhere on this island she'd found a supplier? Someone who could provide her with drugs.

*Paris!*

The youth's name sprang instantly into her mind. As far as she was aware, Sophie hadn't seen the young Greek since he'd piloted the motor cruiser that had brought them to the island, but what if she had? What had he said to her while Paige had been recovering from the journey? What arrangements had they made to see one another again?

If they had.

Paige sighed. Was she overreacting? Just because Sophie wasn't in her room, that was no reason to think she'd left the house. For heaven's sake, it could be that she'd gone to the kitchen because she was hungry. It might be something as simple as foraging for a snack.

Or it might not.

Paige wrapped her arms about her waist and walked over to the windows. Beyond, the lights of Agios Petros glittered in the distance. How far was it to the small town? Two or three kilometres, at least. Too far for Sophie to walk. And, despite the island's idyllic reputation, too dangerous.

She couldn't have gone there, Paige reassured herself firmly. Sophie might enjoy working out, but she wasn't the type to walk anywhere she didn't have to. She couldn't drive so there was no way she could have borrowed one of Nikolas's vehicles. No, she had to be in the house. But where?

She'd wait, she determined, glad to have come to a decision. Sooner or later, Sophie was bound to come back. When she did, Paige intended to give her a piece of her mind for frightening her like this. If she'd intended to leave her room, why couldn't she have told Paige where she was going?

But that aroused more trepidation than it pacified. Paige realised she was beginning to face the possibility that her sister might have left the house. And if she had, if she'd gone into town by some means Paige could only guess at, what was she doing there? And, more importantly, who was she with?

Deciding to wait in Sophie's room instead of her own, just in case she came back without her knowledge, Paige left her room again and walked towards her sister's door. As she did so, she heard voices—both male and female— echoing from the landing at the top of the stairs.

She'd run back along the corridor before she realised they were speaking in Greek, and she was brought up short at the sight of Nikolas and Ariadne, sharing what appeared to be an intimate embrace. The girl was in his arms, her face pressed confidingly into the open V of his jacket, and Nikolas was comforting her, his hand moving soothingly over her slim shoulders.

Paige was glad she was wearing rubber-soled shoes. She'd taken to wearing casual clothes in the evening, trousers or shorts teamed with a pretty blouse or a sleeveless top. This evening she was dressed in a violet silk vest, matching shorts and deck shoes. Not exactly the outfit to impress anyone, but Sophie had told her that these days anything you liked to wear was 'cool'.

Sophie...

Paige shrank back against the wall, hoping they hadn't seen her. Obviously now was not the moment to ask Nikolas if he knew where her sister was. Never mind the fact that seeing him with Ariadne had been a shock, and had reminded her of the outrageous things Ariadne had claimed about her guardian, she had no right to interrupt them. God knew, maybe what Ariadne had said hadn't been so outrageous, after all. Maybe Nikolas was grooming his ward to be his wife.

It was too much. Paige felt as if she was in danger of throwing up. First Sophie; now this. How many more surprises was she supposed to stand before her system rebelled in the most fundamental way?

Shaking her head to clear the slight dizziness that had gripped her, she prepared to make a discreet retreat. But before she could move Nikolas saw her. 'Paige!' he exclaimed, putting Ariadne away from him. He stared at her across the width of the landing. 'Is something wrong?'

'I— No.' Paige straightened away from the wall. She couldn't confide her worries to him now.

'Then why are you so pale?' Leaving Ariadne's side, he crossed the landing to stand in front of her. His brows drew together and his voice softened with unbearable kindness. 'You can tell me. Are you not feeling well?'

'Oh—'

Ridiculously, Paige wanted to cry suddenly. She'd been so anxious and now Nikolas was offering to share the burden with her. But she couldn't ask him for help, not when it would entail too many explanations she didn't want to give.

'Nikolas!' Ariadne's petulant tone drew his attention. 'What is the matter? I thought you were going to bed.'

'You go to bed, Ariadne.' Whatever he'd planned to do, Nikolas was not prepared to be disobeyed.

'But Nikolas—'

'I said, go to bed,' he retorted, his words inflexible. 'I will speak to you in the morning, *pethi. Kalinihta sas.*'

Paige wanted to leave them to it, but Nikolas had braced a hand against the wall and it would have meant ducking under it to go back the way she'd come. But she had no desire for Ariadne to think she was afraid to speak to her guardian, or that Nikolas should think she had some reason for running away.

Ariadne left them with obvious reluctance. Apart from anything else, Paige was sure she was curious to know what was going on. Which was another reason not to confide in Nikolas. She wouldn't give Ariadne any more ammunition to use against them.

'Now?' Nikolas looked interrogatively at her. 'We are alone, so perhaps you will tell me why you came rushing along the corridor as you did? Were you looking for me? Had you heard my voice as I was comforting Ariadne? It is the anniversary of her parents' deaths today. She was upset, so I took her out for dinner.' His lips compressed briefly. 'There: that is my explanation. Will you satisfy my curiosity now?'

Paige squared her shoulders. 'I didn't want to speak to you,' she said, despising herself for not being honest about it. 'I—I was looking—looking for my room.'

'I am sure you know where your room is perfectly well,'

replied Nikolas flatly. 'You will have to do better than that if you expect me to believe you.'

'I don't care whether you believe me or not.' Paige didn't have the will to argue with him. 'I'm tired. If you don't mind, I'd like to go back to my room.'

'Ah, but you don't know where that is,' he reminded her, mocking her confusion. 'Come along. I'll take you there. It's this way.'

He indicated the corridor that Ariadne had followed moments earlier, but when he stood back for her to precede him she refused to go. 'My room is this way,' she said wearily, gesturing behind her. 'All right. I wasn't looking for my room. Can I go to bed now?'

Nikolas's nostrils flared. 'If you were not looking for your room, what were you looking for? Let me guess: Sophie. Am I correct?'

'How do you—?' she began, and then stopped when she realised she'd betrayed herself. 'Very well. Sophie's not in her room. I think she must have gone downstairs.'

'Downstairs?'

Nikolas was unconvinced, and Paige sighed in frustration. 'I don't know where she is,' she admitted honestly. 'Perhaps she wanted a drink.'

'And have you asked Kiria Papandreiu?'

'Of course I haven't asked Kiria Papandreiu.'

'Then let's do it.' Nikolas slipped his hand around her wrist. 'Come along. I'm sure she will still be about.'

'This isn't necessary,' muttered Paige as they descended the stairs together. And then, because he'd ignored her, she added provokingly, 'Aren't you afraid Ariadne will wonder what's going on?'

'I will treat that remark with the contempt it deserves,' he said, and she knew a ridiculous lightening of her spirits. 'Ariadne is my ward, Paige. Not my keeper.'

'If you say so.' Paige tried to hide her relief.

'I do.' Nikolas glanced back at her briefly and then released her wrist as they reached the hall. 'Come: we will see if my housekeeper has seen or heard from your sister. If not…' His mouth compressed. 'I suppose we will have to think again.'

Kiria Papandreiu's apartments adjoined the kitchens. An enclosed walkway gave access to a pretty, creeper-hung building that was completely self-contained. Whitewashed walls, in the Greek style, thick and receptive to the temperature, gave access to a small parlour, and the old woman came to see what they wanted, wrapping a flannel dressing gown about her angular form.

As Paige had half expected, she insisted she knew nothing of Sophie's whereabouts. Nikolas spoke to her in their own language to save time, so Paige could only understand a word here and there. Then, as they were leaving, she came after them, whispering something that was inaudible to Paige in her employer's ear, causing Nikolas to scowl consideringly as they walked back into the villa.

As soon as they reached the kitchen, Paige turned to him. 'What is it?' she demanded. 'What did she say? I know she said something about Sophie. I can see it in your face.'

Nikolas was silent until they'd entered the reception hall. Once they were there, he stopped and looked down at Paige with guarded eyes. 'Kiria Papandreiu thinks your sister may have gone to Petros. If she has, I will find her. Go to bed, *aghapita*. I will see that she tells you all about it in the morning.'

Paige took a step back. 'Petros?' she echoed. 'She's gone into Agios Petros?'

All her worst fears were compounded when Nikolas inclined his head. 'It's possible,' he said, but she knew he was only playing down the situation to reassure her. He glanced towards the salon. 'Would you like a drink first to help you sleep?'

'A drink?' Paige gasped. 'Do you think I can go to bed not knowing where she is or what she's doing? Sophie doesn't know her way around Agios Petros. Anything could have happened.'

'I think not.' Nikolas considered his words before continuing. 'It is possible that this is not the first time she has—how would you put it?—absconded, *ohi*?'

'What do you mean?' She frowned. 'What else did Kiria Papandreiu say?'

Nikolas sighed. 'Perhaps I am wrong,' he said, lifting his shoulders, but she was sure he knew something he wasn't telling her. He paused. '*Poli kala*, if you will not go to bed, I suggest you stay here. I will be as quick as I can—'

'I'm coming with you,' said Paige emphatically. 'I have no intention of letting you go alone.'

Nikolas's brows arched. 'Even though I do not wish it?' He shook his head. 'I have a mobile phone in the car, Paige. Wouldn't it be more sensible if one of us stayed here in case she returns?'

Paige expelled a frustrated breath. He had a point. But the idea of hanging about here while Nikolas went into town was not appealing.

'Do—do you have any idea where she might be?' she asked at last, without answering him, and he shrugged.

'At one of the tavernas near the quay, maybe.' He was thoughtful. 'There is music there, and alcohol. I assume that is what you are concerned about? The fact that Sophie might be drinking and she's under age?'

Paige felt the heat rising up her throat and prayed he wouldn't notice. 'Well—yes,' she murmured, consoling herself with the thought that it wasn't a lie. It just wasn't the whole truth, that was all. 'I just wish I knew how she's got to town, if indeed that's where she is.'

'Ah.' Nikolas looked slightly discomfited now. 'Well, I may have the answer to that as well.'

'You do?' Paige was confused, and he nodded.

'Um—Kiria Papandreiu said something about a *motosik-*

*leta*, a motorbike?' he replied ruefully. 'Does Sophie know someone who rides a—motorbike?'

'Only Paris, perhaps,' said Paige at once, and saw Nikolas's expression darken with sudden impatience.

'Paris Gavril?' he demanded, and Paige felt as if she'd betrayed a confidence of sorts.

'I don't know his surname,' she confessed awkwardly. 'He's the young man you sent to meet us at Piraeus.'

'I sent no young man to meet you at Piraeus,' retorted Nikolas, obviously annoyed now. 'I asked Michaelis Gavril to meet you. Paris is his younger son.'

# CHAPTER TWELVE

'OH.' PAIGE caught her lip between her teeth. 'Well…' She didn't want to get anybody into trouble unnecessarily. 'It was only a thought. He may not be involved.'

'Even though he does drive a Japanese Suzuki?' suggested Nikolas drily. He balled his fists in frustration. 'And you think Sophie may be with him?'

'Well, she might. They seemed to get on awfully well on—on the boat.' She felt guilty for not having foreseen this complication. 'I'm sorry…'

'It is not your fault.' Nikolas gave her an impatient look. 'You weren't to know that your sister might be flattered by Paris's—I have to say rather practised—attentions.' He frowned. 'I wonder if his father knows what's going on? Somehow, I doubt it.'

Paige felt awful. 'Sophie's not an innocent, you know,' she murmured, and then could have cut her tongue out at her particular choice of words. 'That is—she's fairly—streetwise, you know.'

'Unlike her sister,' observed Nikolas flatly. 'Thank you, Paige, but I didn't need to be reminded of that. I hadn't forgotten our experiences, I assure you. But perhaps it explains why she liked Paris, *ne*?'

Paige groaned. 'I didn't mean—'

'Of course you didn't.' But he was practical. 'Ah, well, let us return to the matter in hand.' He hesitated. 'Tell me, has Sophie ever done anything like this before?'

'Like what?' she asked warily. Then, 'She's a teenager, Nikolas. Teenagers do this kind of thing. Or they do if they feel they have a grudge against life.'

'A grudge against life?' She should have known he'd take her up on that, and she didn't have a glib explanation.

'Oh—you know,' she murmured helplessly. 'The fact that Daddy died without making—adequate provision for her future.'

'Or for yours,' Nikolas appended gently, and to her dismay his hand came beneath her chin and tilted her face up to his. 'Was it really worth it?'

'Worth what?' Paige was confused. 'I don't know what you—'

'Denying that we had any future together,' he said astonishingly. 'I know your father was angry with me for thwarting his plans, but I had thought you were different from him.' His lips twisted regretfully. 'Was I wrong? Had you been in his confidence all along?'

'You're mad!' Paige jerked her chin out of his hand and crossed her arms tightly about her waist. 'I don't know why you're bringing that up. Sophie's missing and I'm going out of my mind!'

'As am I,' said Nikolas harshly. 'And you're right. Now is not the time to indulge in old grievances from the past. But that time will come, Paige; depend on it. I have no intention of letting you leave here without telling you exactly what your father said.'

Paige's nerves tightened, but although he looked as if he would have liked to say more he moved instead towards the door. 'The number of the car phone is beside the phone in the library,' he said, stepping out into the jasmine-scented evening. 'If she comes back before I do, let me know.'

'I will.' Paige followed him onto the verandah. Then, because this was Nikolas and, whatever he said, she still had feelings for him, she added, 'Take care.'

His lips twitched. 'I will,' he said drily, coiling his length behind the wheel of the four-by-four that was parked outside. He put the car into gear. 'Try not to worry.'

The car began to roll forward, but before he'd gone more than a few yards Paige heard the unmistakable whine of a motorcycle accelerating up from the road. Nikolas must have heard it, too, because he braked, the red bulbs glowing briefly before he cut his engine and his lights.

Paige pulled the door closed behind her, to prevent the hall lights from betraying her presence, but she needn't have worried. Long before the motorbike reached the forecourt, it veered away into the trees, its headlight arcing briefly across the walls of the villa before being engulfed by the lush vegetation.

Nikolas vaulted out of the car. 'They've gone round to the back,' he said, starting after them. 'Wait here.'

There were a nerve-racking few moments. Paige waited until he had been swallowed up by the darkness of the rose pergola before turning and going back into the house. Closing the door behind her, she hurried across the hall and along the corridor that led to the back of the villa. Concealed lighting along the tops of the walls meant she didn't have to switch on any lights as she went, but that didn't stop her from letting out a little cry of surprise when a black-clad figure burst out of the shadows and into her involuntary embrace.

'Let go of— Paige!'

Sophie's shocked exclamation was reassuring, but Paige's relief was short-lived. The realisation that her fears about her sister had been justified overcame any momentary satisfaction at finding she was unharmed, and when she could get hold of her properly she gave her an angry shake.

'Where the hell have you been?' she demanded, not even noticing that Sophie was wearing her black shirt and black jeans—clothes her sister would have normally shunned like the plague, but which were obviously more suitable than a miniskirt for riding a motorbike. 'How long has this been going on?'

'Not now, Paige.' Sophie was agitated, trying to free

herself, glancing back apprehensively over her shoulder. 'Let's talk about this in the morning, right? Not now.'

'Why not now?' Paige wouldn't release her. 'So you can have the time to think up a convenient excuse as to why you weren't in your room? The game's up, Sophie. I saw the motorbike. Paris's motorbike. So don't try to deny it.'

If she'd had any doubts about Nikolas's interpretation of events, they were stifled by the look of shocked discovery in her sister's face. 'How did you—?' she began, and then evidently decided she didn't have time to discuss it now. 'Look, all right. I've been out with Paris, yeah? But I think someone else saw us.' She glanced over her shoulder again. 'Why don't we get out of here before whoever it is puts two and two together and comes after us?'

'After us?' said Paige coldly. 'There is no *us*, Sophie.'

'Okay.' Sophie's face hardened. 'Have it your own way. But how long do you think your job with Petronides will last if he finds out I've been sneaking out every night to meet one of his own employees?'

'He knows,' remarked Nikolas, appearing from the same direction as Sophie. Dark and disturbing, he moved into the light, and Paige saw her sister give her a wary look. 'I have just had a very interesting conversation with your—what shall I say?—your accomplice, *ne*?'

Sophie wrenched herself out of Paige's grasp. 'Oh, I get it,' she said, looking from her sister to Nikolas and back again with resentful eyes. 'The gang of two. Or should I say the gang of three? I knew I couldn't trust that—that little bitch not to say anything.'

Paige's eyes had widened in disbelief, but it was Nikolas who spoke. 'You are claiming that Ariadne knew of this?' he demanded. 'No. That cannot be.'

'Don't you think so?' Sophie was defiant now, propping her hands on her hips, and regarding them both with equal contempt. 'Well, she did. Her room overlooks the olive grove where we—where Paris usually drops me off. She was waiting for me one night when I let myself into the villa.'

Paige was horrified. 'What did she say?'

'What do you think?' Sophie gave a careless shrug. 'I'd have said she was jealous only she's got something going on with him, hasn't she?' She jerked a thumb towards Nikolas. 'She told me all about it.' Her mouth curled. 'They're lovers. Or that's what she said.'

Paige caught her breath. 'Sophie—'

'It's true, Paige. Why d'you think she agreed not to tell you what I was doing? She said as long as I stopped making cracks about their relationship she'd keep her mouth shut. But now—'

'Ariadne told us nothing,' said Paige, through parched lips. She turned disbelieving eyes in Nikolas's direction. 'Is this true?' she added faintly, and even Sophie looked staggered at the presumption of the question.

She was even more shocked when Nikolas said flatly, 'Do you believe it is?' and Paige didn't immediately reply.

'For God's sake, Paige!' she exclaimed impatiently then. 'Of course it's true. She gave me all the sordid details. It's been going on for ages. Don't let him make a fool of you just because you're afraid to lose this job.'

'I'm not afraid of losing my job,' said Paige steadily, still looking at Nikolas. 'I think you should go to bed, Sophie. We'll talk about this in the morning.'

'No.' Nikolas spoke again. 'No, Paige, I want her to hear what you really think. Now. Not in the morning. Do you really believe I am having a relationship with my ward?'

Paige took a deep breath. 'I—I wouldn't have thought so,' she said weakly, and Sophie gave an angry exclamation.

'You're crazy,' she said. 'You should have heard what she has to say. All about what they do in bed, stuff like that.'

Paige sighed. 'Sophie, anyone can make up stories of

that kind. You only need to buy a video; read a book. These days nothing is left to the imagination.'

'All right, then.' Sophie was desperate to find a way to convince her. 'Why don't you ask Ariadne? I'll go and wake her up, shall I? That is, if she is asleep yet.' Sophie eyes swept Nikolas with a scornful look. 'But you'd know that better than me.'

'Sophie!'

Paige was tired of her sister's constant provocation, but it was Nikolas who chose to speak again. 'I intend to ask Ariadne myself,' he said. 'But not tonight. In the morning. Contrary to your beliefs, Sophie, I know nothing of my ward's sleeping habits.'

Sophie grunted. 'You would say that.'

'Yes, I would.' Nikolas's patience was thinning, and even Sophie shrank before the grim determination in his face. 'I intend to get to the bottom of this. And speaking to Ariadne is the very least I intend to do.'

Sophie hunched her shoulders. 'I'd like to be present at that interview,' she muttered sulkily, and to Paige's surprise Nikolas nodded again.

'You will be,' he promised her. 'Both of you. You can depend on it.'

'Yeah, right.' Sophie shifted uneasily. 'When you've had a chance to prime her about what to say.'

'I have no intention of priming her,' retorted Nikolas shortly. 'As I hope your sister knows, I am an honourable man. When Ariadne's parents were killed and I was appointed her guardian, I was well aware that as she grew older certain arrangements would have to be made. That is one of the reasons why I asked Paige to become her companion, even though I realise chaperons are considered passé in this day and age.' His lips twisted. 'Or perhaps not.'

Paige shook her head. 'There's no need for this, Nikolas,' she murmured unhappily. 'You don't have to justify the situation to me.' She turned to her sister. 'I believe him, Sophie. I know he's not lying. So let this be an end of it. I don't want to hear any more accusations from you.'

Sophie's expression was sardonic now. 'You know?' she countered sarcastically. 'How do you know?'

Paige expelled a weary breath. 'I just do.'

Sophie blinked. And then comprehension seemed to dawn. 'You mean—oh, God! That's what all this is about. You're having an affair with him, too.'

'Don't be ridiculous—'

'As a matter of fact, your sister and I did have an affair four years ago,' Nikolas interrupted Paige steadily. 'She and your father were my guests here and on board my yacht. I'm not sure she would wish you to know this, but there it is. I think you could say that she knows me— intimately.'

Sophie's jaw dropped. 'I don't believe this.'

'What don't you believe?' Nikolas enquired.

'This. All of it. Paige never said anything about an affair to me.'

'Why would she?' Nikolas's tone was mild. 'Your father did not approve of our relationship. Paige was obviously unable—or unwilling—to ignore his wishes.'

'You're saying Daddy knew about it?' Sophie stared at him.

'He learned about it afterwards,' Nikolas amended. 'I can tell you on good authority, he was not pleased. Unfortunately, Paige and I had had little time to get to know one another before she left the island. I did try to reach her after she returned to London but she never re- turned my calls.'

*Returned his calls?*

It was Paige's turn to look startled now. What calls? she wanted to say. There had never been any calls from him.

'I expect, like her father, she blamed me for what had

happened,' Nikolas continued ruefully. 'I admit my behaviour was not inclined to win her trust.'

Sophie shook her head. 'So that's why you gave her this job?'

'No.' Nikolas denied that, much to Paige's surprise. 'I offered her the job to help out a friend.'

'A friend!'

Sophie snorted, but Nikolas was implacable. 'Yes, a friend,' he agreed. 'I knew she would never ask for my help, no matter how difficult things had become since your father's death.'

'You know about that?'

'It was hardly a secret,' he said levelly, glancing at Paige, and she realised he had no idea how confused she felt. 'In my country, in times of stress, we try to help one another. Offering Paige the job was my way of atoning for the past.'

*Atoning!*

Paige just wanted this conversation to be over. She wanted to go to her room and think about what Nikolas had said. But, whatever he'd meant, nothing could alter the fact that he'd regretted what had happened. Though not as much as she had, she thought wryly.

Sophie lifted her shoulders now, turning to her sister with resentment as well as resignation in her eyes. 'So that's why you were so keen to come here,' she said accusingly. 'It wasn't because of me at all.'

Paige didn't ever remember telling Sophie that she was keen to come here. But she knew better than to call her on it right at this moment. Sophie was like a loose cannon, and in her present mood there was no telling what she might say next.

But she'd forgotten that Nikolas was there, too, and his brows drew together at Sophie's words. 'Because of you?' he asked, evidently curious, and Sophie seemed to realise she had a means of turning the tables on Paige.

'Yeah, me,' she said airily, daring Paige to contradict

her. 'She wasn't too keen on the gang I was running round with back home. Didn't she tell you why she was so keen to get me out of London? She was afraid I was in danger of becoming an addict. Just because our dotty old aunt found a gram of heroin in my knicker drawer.'

# CHAPTER THIRTEEN

PAIGE had already been served her breakfast when Sophie appeared. The young girl looked heavy-eyed and apprehensive, and Paige guessed she must have disturbed her when she'd opened her door.

She'd looked into her sister's room before coming downstairs. But Sophie had appeared to be sound asleep, and although she felt no sympathy for her this morning Paige had decided not to awaken her. Besides, it had crossed her mind that Nikolas might ask her to leave at the earliest opportunity, and she'd decided she'd prefer her humiliation to be a private, rather than a public, thing.

Which was why she'd been glad Ariadne wasn't around either. Right now, she didn't think she could look at the Greek girl without her resentment showing. Ariadne might not be totally to blame for what had happened the night before, but without her fabrications Sophie would never have dared confront Nikolas as she had.

Or provoke such a damning evocation of their shared past, Paige conceded painfully. She had no idea why Nikolas had felt the need to acquaint her sister with the truth about their relationship, but he had. Yet even that had paled beside Sophie's malicious revelations. She couldn't believe Nikolas would want her to continue as Ariadne's companion after what he'd learnt last night.

The sad thing was, she'd thought she was making such good progress. She and Ariadne had had their differences, goodness knew, but on the whole she'd believed they'd all adapted amazingly well in the circumstances. How foolish she'd been! Ariadne had been feeding her sister lies about

Nikolas and Sophie had been spending most evenings with Paris, and laughing at her behind her back.

Of course, Sophie had denied it. The laughing-behind-her-back bit, at least. When they'd eventually reached her room the night before, she'd sworn she'd never intended to hurt Paige. But spending every evening at the villa had been a dead bore, she'd protested. Agios Petros was fun. All she and Paris had done was visit a few tavernas. There'd been disco music and dancing, but no drugs, she'd insisted. And she'd never drunk more than a couple of beers.

*A couple of beers!* Paige had had a hard time getting her head around the fact that Sophie had been drinking alcohol. She was under age, after all. Apart from the fact that she knew it was wrong, she could have faced conviction or worse. But Sophie's face had taken on its wooden expression at that point, and she'd known that her protests were going over the girl's head. Besides, Sophie had been agitating to go back to London for as long as they'd been on the island. Whatever happened, she had nothing to lose.

But Paige had.

She'd refused to discuss her association with Nikolas. Despite Sophie's exhortations that she was no better than she was, she hadn't been drawn. But it would come, she thought ruefully, looking at Sophie's mutinous expression. And sooner rather than later if Sophie had her way.

'Sleep well?' she asked now, sheltering behind a cup of coffee, and Sophie sniffed before helping herself to a glass of freshly squeezed orange juice.

'You don't have to make small talk,' she said. 'I know I'm in the doghouse. But I'm not to blame if you told lies about why you decided to take this job.'

Paige shrugged. 'I'd rather not discuss it.'

'I bet you wouldn't.' Sophie glowered at her across the table. Then she shook her head. 'I don't believe it, you know. You and Petronides getting it on.'

'Don't use that expression.'

Paige's tone was sharp, but Sophie seemed indifferent to any sensitivities her sister might have. 'Okay,' she said. 'It's hard to believe he'd want to—have sex with someone like you.'

'Why?' Paige had to ask. She found her self-respect was not totally shredded after all.

'Well, like—he's a millionaire, right?' said Sophie, grimacing. 'I mean, okay, you're not bad-looking, but he could have any woman he wanted.'

'And does, probably,' said Paige tightly, wanting to change the subject now. 'Anyway, you'd better start packing after you've had breakfast.'

'Start packing?' Sophie looked stunned. 'Oh, no. We're not leaving!'

'Well, what did you expect after you practically bragged about possessing drugs last night?'

'But it's not true.' Sophie groaned. 'The only thing I've tried is grass. The heroin wasn't mine. It was Justine's.' She heaved a sigh. 'She asked me to keep it for her the last time she came to the house.'

'Justine's?' Paige stared at her. 'Justine Lowery?' The girl was one of Sophie's friends from boarding-school. She was Judge Lowery's daughter. 'Heavens, I can imagine her father's reaction if he finds out.'

'But he won't find out, will he?' Sophie was dismissive. 'You emptied it into the loo. She was pretty miffed when I phoned her and told her. I doubt if she'll ever trust me again.'

'Thank heavens for small mercies,' said Paige drily, though she was dreading what might happen when they got back to England. To begin with, she was going to have to ask Aunt Ingrid if they could stay with her for a few days until Paige could find them an alternative. But even if Nikolas paid her for the three weeks she'd been here it wasn't going to be easy to find a flat.

'Anyway, Petronides hasn't asked you to leave, has he?' Sophie persisted, but before Paige could give an answer Ariadne appeared. In cropped trousers and a T-shirt she looked particularly complacent this morning, and Paige sought refuge in her coffee cup again as she sat down.

'Good morning,' she said, including both of them in her greeting. 'I am sorry if I am late. I must have overslept.'

'Didn't Nikolas disturb you when he got up?' enquired Paige drily, drawing a startled look from her sister. 'Kiria Papandreiu said he had something to eat earlier on.'

'How am I supposed to know where Nikolas is?' Ariadne glanced at her warily. 'I have no idea what time he got up.'

'You do surprise me.' Paige wasn't inclined to be charitable this morning, and she was pleased that Sophie was keeping her mouth shut. She guessed her sister was stunned by her uncharacteristic bravado. 'I thought you told Sophie that you and your guardian were having an affair.'

Ariadne went scarlet. If Paige had nurtured any doubts about Nikolas's sincerity, they were dispelled by the guilty look on the other girl's face. 'She—she told you that?' she stammered, her throat muscles moving convulsively as she swallowed. Then she seemed to decide she had no choice but to bluff it out. 'What happened? Did you find out she's been going into Agios Petros every night?'

'She told me about that, yes.' But Paige was not about to explain how she had found out. 'And about the little bargain you supposedly made. Does your guardian know you're spreading these stories about him?'

'They're not stories.' Ariadne tossed her head. 'I'm glad she's told you what I said, but I really don't think it's anything to do with you.'

Paige caught her lower lip between her teeth. 'But it's not true, is it?' she persisted softly. 'You made it up because Sophie was teasing you about not having any friends.'

'No!' Ariadne looked at Sophie's smug face, and Paige

realised she'd never admit anything in the younger girl's presence. 'It's true. I expect you'll find it hard to believe, but Nikolas and I have been lovers for months.'

'You lie!'

Paige didn't know which of the three of them was most surprised by Nikolas's sudden interjection. She'd thought they were alone on the patio but now she saw that Nikolas had been sitting on one of the loungers beside the pool all along. He rose from his chair, which had been concealed by one of the striped umbrellas, and she saw he was still wearing the formal clothes he'd had on the night before. He'd removed his tie and his dress shirt was open at the neck and judging by the stubble of beard that shadowed his jawline, she guessed he'd been there all night.

'You are lying,' he repeated, climbing the steps from the pool deck and crossing the patio towards them. 'Sophie told me what you had said, but I still hoped that she might have misunderstood you. But there was no misunderstanding, was there, Ariadne? You disgust me. You have sullied our relationship by making claims that are an embarrassment at best and at worst a crude attempt to destroy my reputation.'

'No...' Ariadne scrambled to her feet. 'No, that's not true.' She wrung her hands in anguish. 'Nikolas, do not be angry with me, please. You do not know what it has been like for me.' She cast Paige's sister an agonised look. 'She—she made me do it. Sophie is always making fun of me. I had to say something to—to make her stop.'

Nikolas was unmoved. 'So you chose to slander me.'

'No.' Ariadne gazed up at him with frantic eyes. 'She said she didn't know why I put up with you telling me what to do, so I let her think that—that we were—more than friends.'

'You let her think we were lovers,' Nikolas corrected her contemptuously. He folded his arms and regarded her with such a look of distaste on his dark face that Paige almost found it in her heart to feel sorry for the girl herself.

'Well—perhaps.' Ariadne took a deep breath and then added imploringly, 'It is not so incredible, is it? I will be old enough to get married next year.'

'Not to me,' said Nikolas heavily, and the girl stepped back at the bitterness in his voice. 'In fact, I think it would be more convenient if you became a boarder at the convent from now on. I am sure I could arrange for them to accommodate you for the rest of the summer and school will begin again in September, as you know.'

Ariadne was horrified. 'You don't mean that, Nikolas—'

'I do.'

'But—but you said I could stay here until school starts again.'

'That was before you revealed this rather unpleasant side to your nature,' he retorted coldly. 'How do you think I feel knowing you have been entertaining such thoughts?'

Ariadne's mouth was open. She was breathing noisily and Paige guessed that at any minute she was going to burst into tears. It made her feel uncomfortable being a party to the girl's humiliation. Even Sophie wasn't gloating over it, though her sister guessed she'd say that Ariadne had brought it all upon herself.

Coming to a decision, Paige put her hands on the table. 'I think, if you'll excuse us...' she began, but that was as far as she got.

'Stay.' Nikolas's tone was sharp, but he tempered it with, 'Please.' And, although she was sure Ariadne wouldn't thank her for it, she sank back into her chair.

Sophie felt no such obligation, however. With a roll of her eyes at her sister, she sidled off into the house. 'I'll start packing,' she said, and Paige wondered if she realised how provocative her words sounded. Apparently, as far as Sophie was concerned, Ariadne was on her way back to school.

'You said you'd always take care of me,' Ariadne cried now, seeming incapable of understanding that by defaming his name she'd done something totally unforgivable in Nikolas's eyes. 'When Mama and Papa died, you said I could always depend on your support for—for everything. You told me you considered it a privilege that Papa had made you my—my—'

'Guardian,' said Nikolas bleakly. 'I was proud that your father considered me a suitable substitute for him. I have tried to behave as a parent would, Ariadne. I loved you as a father. Nothing else.'

Tears began streaming down Ariadne's cheeks. 'But you said I was beautiful.' She sniffed. 'That night—that night I wore Mama's dress, you said I looked a lot like her.'

'And so you did.' Nikolas spoke wearily now. 'You do. You are her daughter, Ariadne. But please don't confuse admiration for—for love.'

The girl gasped. 'You don't love me?'

'I have never loved you as a man loves the woman he wants to marry.'

'And—and you're sending me away—'

'I'm sending you back to school.' Nikolas's lean face was etched with tiredness. 'Do not think to change my mind, Ariadne. I suggest you spend the time between now and September deciding which courses you would like to take next year when you enrol in college.'

'In college!'

Ariadne's sobs grew louder, and casting a pain-filled look at Paige, she turned and rushed through the French windows into the house. Her shoulders were hunched and she looked so young suddenly that Paige was moved by her plight, and despite Nikolas's expression she got determinedly to her feet.

'I'll go after her,' she said, even though she was not at all convinced that Ariadne would want any sympathy from her. But she had to do something. The girl had looked so desperate when she'd rushed away.

'Paige.' As she'd half expected, Nikolas's voice detained her. 'I want to speak to you,' he said. He rubbed a rueful hand over the rough stubble on his jaw. 'After I've cleaned up.'

'Very well.' Paige could guess what he wanted to talk about. If he was sending Ariadne back to school, there was no job for her here. If indeed there had been after last night, she conceded flatly. 'I'll be in my room,' she said, moving her shoulders in a uncertain gesture. 'Or Ariadne's. Although I doubt if she'll welcome any help from me.'

In fact she caught up with the girl as she was climbing the stairs. Her steps had slowed considerably, and, judging by the hopeful expression she turned on Paige, she must have expected her guardian would come after her. Her mouth pursed when she realised her mistake, but for once she had no ready retort to make. Instead, she looked at the other girl rather warily, as if she suspected Paige was here to gloat.

'Are you all right?'

Paige knew it was a silly question in the circumstances, but it was difficult to think of anything else to say. At least Ariadne had stopped crying. She confined herself to an occasional hiccough as they reached the landing on the first floor.

'As if you care,' she muttered at last, but there was no heat in the words now. Paige realised this must have been a salutary lesson for her. She had obviously believed she could say and do anything she liked and Nikolas would never turn against her.

'We all make mistakes,' said Paige with deliberate optimism, thinking that she'd made more than most. 'Look, don't quote me on this but I'm sure in time Nikolas will forgive you. He's angry right now, but he'll get over it. If you keep out of his way, he'll probably allow you to stay here until school starts again.'

Ariadne's eyes widened. 'Do you really think so?'

'Well, it's a possibility,' said Paige, unwilling to say any more than that. 'Why don't you go and wash your face and brush your hair and then get some breakfast? You'll feel heaps better after you've had something to eat.'

'All right.' Ariadne hesitated. Then, pressing her palms together, she said, 'Thank you.'

Paige shrugged. 'No problem.'

'No, I mean it.' Ariadne clearly wanted to say something more and, although Paige wasn't sure it was justified, she added, 'I think you understand Nikolas better than I do.'

Paige gave a wry smile. 'I wouldn't say that.'

'I would.' Ariadne took a deep breath. 'He always listens to you.'

'Does he?' Paige doubted that, and she chided herself for the little germ of suspicion that flowered at Ariadne's professed confidence in her. 'Well, don't speak too soon. I don't have any influence on his decisions.'

'But you could have,' urged Ariadne, encouraging Paige to accompany her to her room. 'If—if you told him how sorry I am; how much I wish this had never happened. That it was all a mistake. That I never intended him to find out.'

'Look, Ariadne…' Paige halted, not prepared to be drawn into an alliance with her. 'Quit while you're ahead. I've told you what I think, but I can't fight your battles for you. It's up to you to prove to your guardian that you're sorry. And telling him that you never intended him to find out about what you were saying is not going to do it.'

'Then what?'

Ariadne looked as if she would have liked to continue their conversation, but Paige had had enough. Giving the younger girl's hand a comforting squeeze, she started back the way they'd come. She just hoped Sophie was in her room, doing what she'd promised. The last thing she needed right now was another confrontation with her.

Sophie was in her room, but she wasn't packing. She was sitting out on the balcony, and she tilted her head enquiringly when Paige came in. 'Well?' she said carelessly. 'Did you sort it out? Hey, I thought Petronides was going to hit her, didn't you? Poor Ariadne! She must have wanted to die when she realised he'd been listening to her all along.'

'Yes—well, it's nothing to do with us,' said Paige shortly, reminded of how the whole sorry mess had come to light. 'And I thought you said you were going to do your packing.'

'We're not really leaving, are we?' Sophie gazed up at her with disbelieving eyes.

'What else did you expect? You heard Nikolas say he was sending Ariadne back to the convent.'

'Well, yes, but that was in the heat of the moment.' Sophie sighed. 'He'll listen to you,' she added wheedlingly. 'Couldn't you talk him round?'

'No, I couldn't.' Paige found she resented the fact that both girls thought they could use her to get what they wanted. 'In any case, I thought you were keen to get back to London.'

'I was.' Sophie was sulky. 'But that was before—before—'

'Before you started going into Agios Petros every night?' Paige was caustic. 'Honestly, Sophie, you really are the limit. You don't think of anyone but yourself.'

'I was just having fun,' protested Sophie, scuffing the toe of her training shoe against the balcony railings. 'I bet you had plenty of fun when you were my age.'

'When I was your age, Mummy was ill and Daddy was going frantic worrying about her,' retorted Paige flatly. 'It was another three years before I met Nikolas, if that's what this is all about.'

Sophie frowned. 'Did you know him for a long time?'

'No.' Paige would have preferred not to talk about him at all. 'Daddy introduced us, and I suppose we knew one another for about two weeks.'

'Two weeks!' Sophie was impressed now. 'Way to go, Paige. You snagged yourself a millionaire in less than fourteen days!' She grinned. 'So—tell me all about it. Was he your first lover? What was he like?'

'You have to be joking!' Paige cringed at the thought of what her sister would think if she told her how gullible she'd been. She headed for the door before Sophie noticed her embarrassment. 'I'm going to start my own packing. I— Nikolas has asked to see me, and I don't need a crystal ball to wonder why.'

# CHAPTER FOURTEEN

SHE decided to give Nikolas an hour to send for her before going to look for him herself. Whatever happened, before she left here she needed to know what he'd meant last night when he'd told Sophie he'd tried to get in touch with her after she and her father had returned to England. He'd probably said it to spare her feelings, but, just in case Sophie asked, she wanted to know the truth.

Or that was what she told herself...

As she took her suitcase out of the closet and set it on the rack, she couldn't help the troubling thought that her father could have intercepted Nikolas's calls. But what if he had? she asked herself defensively. He could only have been protecting her. After the way Nikolas had behaved, her father had had every right to distrust the man.

Or had he...?

She shook the disloyal thought aside and went to get her shoes from the bottom of the tallboy. Her father might not always have been scrupulous in his dealings, but he'd always been entirely honest with her. She was his daughter, for heaven's sake. He'd loved her. Look at the way he'd behaved when he'd found out what Nikolas had done!

She refused to remember the way he'd urged her to treat Nikolas before he'd discovered what had happened. In retrospect, she was sure she must have misunderstood what he'd said. After all, it wasn't the first time he'd asked her to charm one of his clients. He'd been angry with Nikolas and she'd caught the backlash, that was all.

She was putting her underwear into the suitcase when someone knocked at the bedroom door. Guessing it was one of the maids, come to tell her that Nikolas was waiting in his study, she called, *'Beno mesa,'* and continued with her task. But some sixth sense told her it wasn't the maid almost before the door opened, and she wasn't entirely surprised when Nikolas entered the room.

She was surprised when he closed the door behind him, however, and she straightened to face him with wary eyes. It was so totally out of character for him to invade a woman's bedroom uninvited, and she was aware of an anxious tingling in her belly as he leaned back against the panels.

'What are you doing?'

His question was not unexpected even though he must have been able to see perfectly well what she was about. 'I don't know what time the flights leave from Athens,' she said, pushing her thumbs into the waistband of her shorts at the back, and then pulling them out again when she realised it caused her breasts to bead against the thin cotton of her shirt. 'I—I—' She struggled to hide her nervousness. 'Perhaps you could ask Yanis to find out for us.'

'Why would I do that?' Nikolas regarded her with narrowed eyes. He had showered recently, and drops of water sparkled on his dark hair. In a black T-shirt and black cotton trousers, he looked lean and masculine, even if there were lines of weariness etched on his grim face. 'You are not going anywhere.'

Paige blinked. 'But I thought—'

'Yes? What did you think?' Nikolas pushed away from the door. 'That I would allow you to run out on me again as you did before?'

Paige's breath rushed out on a gasp. 'I'd have thought you'd have been glad that I've made it so easy for you,' she said, swallowing her astonishment. 'Is that what you wanted to talk to me about?'

'Partly.' Nikolas was terse. 'But first I wanted to apologise for Ariadne's behaviour. I am afraid I have spoiled her badly. I had no idea that she thought there was more to my affection for her than—well, affection.'

Paige shook her head. 'Young girls often conceive crushes on older men,' she said. Then, seeing his lack of comprehension, she explained, 'I mean puppy love, of course. Infatuation.' She made a helpless gesture. 'She'll get over it.'

'As you did?' asked Nikolas roughly. 'Yes, I suppose you would understand her feelings better than most.'

Paige's jaw dropped. 'I hope you're not implying that what I—what I shared with you was a childish infatuation!' she exclaimed, and he moved his shoulders in a dismissing gesture.

'What else?' he demanded. 'Though I have to say you soon got over it.'

'You don't know anything about my—my feelings,' cried Paige indignantly. And then, because she had to say something in her own defence, she went on, 'I hope you're not going to pretend it meant anything to you. Even if you did tell Sophie that you'd tried to reach me after I went home. What was all that about, by the way? Was it to save my feelings or your own?'

Nikolas's mouth thinned at her deliberate provocation. 'And why would I wish to save your feelings?' he enquired bitterly, and Paige pressed her quivering lips together.

'Indeed,' she said, when she had herself in control again. 'Your own, then. I should have known. I hope you realise that for a few moments you had me actually doubting my father's word.'

'And so you should.' Nikolas spoke hoarsely now. 'I did not wish him dead, Paige, but that man has a lot to answer for.'

'How dare you?' Paige found strength in indignation. 'How dare you defile my father's name? My God, he said you were an unscrupulous bastard, and he was right!'

'Is that what he told you?' Nikolas pulled a wry face. 'Well, what is it the English say? It takes one to know one.'

Paige was incensed at his insensitivity. 'You—you have no right to criticise someone who—who can't defend himself—'

'No? Even when that someone did his best to ruin my reputation?' Nikolas moved closer, and as he did so a stunned expression came over his face. '*Hristo*, he really didn't tell you, did he?'

'Tell me?' Paige stared at him suspiciously. 'Tell me what?'

Nikolas shook his head. 'Yanis swore it was possible but I didn't believe him. I thought he was only saying it to save his own sorry skin.'

'Yanis?' Paige was totally confused. 'Why would Yanis need to save—?'

'Because he was the one who arranged for you to leave the island,' Nikolas broke in impatiently. Then, with a groan, he added, 'Didn't you ever question the fact that I had apparently lost all interest in you when you left?'

Paige shook her head. 'I— No.'

'It meant so little to you?'

Paige flushed. 'I didn't say that.'

'What are you saying, then?' Nikolas gazed at her imploringly. '*Theus*, do you have any idea how I felt when Yanis told me you'd gone?'

'Relieved, I should think.' Paige strove for a glib tone and failed, miserably.

'Desperate,' Nikolas corrected her grimly, stepping forward to grasp her shoulders, and although she made a half-hearted attempt to free herself the anguish in his eyes kept her where she was. 'Paige, didn't you realise how I felt about you, about our relationship? Did it not occur to you that if all I had wanted was to take you to bed, then I would not have respected your innocence for the rest of the time you were on the yacht?'

Paige didn't know how to answer him. 'I—I thought—' *That you were bored with me; that as soon as you discovered how inexperienced I was you regretted getting involved with me...* She shivered suddenly. 'I—I didn't know what to think.'

'Then hear this: I did try to get in touch with you after you returned to London. Several times, in fact.' His lips twisted. 'Until your father told me that I was wasting my time, that there was another man in your life, and that in any case you had only been acting on his instructions.'

'No—'

'Yes.' When she would have stepped back from him, he used her momentary imbalance to jerk her closer. 'Why do you think I was so angry with myself when I betrayed my feelings to you that morning down at the jetty?' he demanded, thrusting his face close to hers. '*Theus*, Paige, for four years I thought you had made a fool of me. My only consolation was that Tennant—your father—hadn't got what he wanted, what he'd traded your innocence to achieve—'

'No...'

But it was a pitiful sound she made, and when he gathered her close against the taut strength of his lean body she trembled in his embrace.

'I didn't betray you, Paige,' he said thickly, his hands sliding up to cradle her skull. 'I fell in love with you. I wanted to marry you. But your father couldn't accept defeat, and although it cost him dearly in the end he destroyed the thing I most desired.'

Paige shook her head. 'Daddy's dead—'

'Do you think I don't know that?' Nikolas spoke bitterly. 'You were right, you know. That day when we had lunch together you understood my motives perfectly. It was no coincidence that I had contacted Price's firm. I'd been waiting four years to have my revenge and when I heard that

Tennant—that your father—was dead I thought any chance of retribution had died with him.'

Paige gazed up at him, aghast. 'Why are you telling me this now?'

'Because I want you to know the truth,' said Nikolas grimly. 'There will be no lies, no half-truths between us. If you decide to forgive me, it will be because you are in possession of all the facts. Not just those I would wish you to know.'

Paige's tongue appeared to moisten her lips, and, as if he couldn't stop himself, Nikolas bent his head to allow their tongues to touch; to mate; to seek an intimacy that had Paige's knees shaking and her hands reaching unsteadily for his waist; for some place she could anchor herself while he took possession of her mouth.

Her senses swam, but, as if he realised that seducing her again was not the answer, Nikolas pulled his mouth away and allowed his thumbs to take its place. '*Gliko,*' he said huskily. 'Very sweet. You have a taste like no other, *agape mou*. But I must not be distracted. I want you to know all my sins, and persuading Price to talk about you was only the least of them.'

Paige shook her head. 'I can't take this in.'

'But you want to?'

She wanted to deny it. She wanted to hold onto the fragile belief that her father had always had her best interests at heart, but it was becoming harder and harder to achieve. And, looking up into Nikolas's dark, anxious face, she knew that being honest with him was more important than hanging onto the crumbling reputation of a dead man.

'Yes,' she said softly. 'Yes, I want to.' And had the satisfaction of seeing the heat of emotion flare in his eyes.

'Very well,' he said, and now she detected a slight tremor in his voice, too. 'So—you must know that it was common knowledge that your father died owing a small fortune, and I watched with interest your efforts to rescue something from the wreck he left behind. Oh, yes.' This, as her eyes widened in shocked denial. 'I am not proud of my actions, *aghapita*, but you must remember I had your father's word that you had been a party to your own seduction.'

Paige shook her head. 'He—he wouldn't say that.'

'Ah, but he did. And more besides.' Nikolas's thumbs caressed her cheeks. 'He wanted me to believe that everything that had happened had been for a purpose; that you did whatever he asked of you, and the reason that you'd left was because you were ashamed that you'd failed.'

Paige blinked. 'But how could you believe that?'

'How could I not, when you consistently refused to return my calls?'

'But I didn't—'

'Know about them? Yes, I realise that now. But at the time I am afraid my anger blinded me to the most transparent of explanations. If I had not been so childishly aggrieved at your apparent behaviour, I would have come to London and had the truth from your own lips.'

Paige took a trembling breath. 'If—if you had come to London, it might not have made any difference,' she murmured unhappily. She hesitated. 'Daddy had told me that you had laughed when he'd expressed his outrage at—at what you'd done. He said you'd told him it was his fault for being fool enough to trust you in the first place.'

Nikolas swore then in his own language, and although Paige didn't understand the words he used she could understand his frustration at the way her father had deceived them both. It was as if Parker Tennant had had no care for his daughter's happiness at all; as if his own loss had destroyed any finer feelings he had once possessed.

After a few moments, Nikolas had himself in control again, but there was a dogged determination in his voice that proved how difficult it was for him to go on. 'So,' he said, his words tight with emotion, 'it is better not to dwell upon the past. Let it be enough to say that we both thought we had our reasons for despising the other, *ohi*?' His eyes searched her pale face. 'But perhaps you can understand now why I was so curious to see how you would handle the situation you found yourself in. Price's behaviour was predictable, of course. I'd known for some time that that young man had an eye to the—to the main chance, *ne*?' His eyes darkened briefly. 'Did you love him?'

Paige gave a rueful sigh. 'You must know I didn't or you wouldn't be asking that question.'

'I hoped,' he said, and, as if unable to resist, he bent his head and brushed a light kiss over the corner of her mouth. 'But I digress. I am nothing if not determined, and if there is something I want I will wait any length of time to get it.'

'But you said—'

'Revenge,' said Nikolas regretfully. 'I wanted revenge, and your vulnerability provided the ideal opportunity.'

'I see.'

'Do you? I wonder.' Nikolas's lips twisted now. 'You have no idea of the torment I went through, wondering if you would prove to be your father's daughter, after all.'

Paige frowned. 'What do you mean?'

'Oh, Paige, surely it must have occurred to you that you could have easily found yourself and Sophie a wealthy protector? You must have met dozens of men in the course of your father's business. I am sure many of them would have been only too glad to—'

'Sell myself, you mean?' Paige stiffened. 'I told you once before, Nikolas—'

'You are not for sale.' He finished the sentence for her. 'I know that now. But at the time…' He sighed. 'I am not proud of the thoughts I had about you, *agape mou*. But when you removed Sophie from her public school and took up residence with your aunt in Islington I knew the time had come for me to act.'

'You knew all that, and yet you still believed that I—'

'No.' Nikolas stopped her there. 'No. Deep down, I suppose I had always known that the creature your father had painted for me bore little resemblance to the beautiful, sensitive woman I had fallen in love with.' He shook his head. 'Yet I still believed that you had betrayed me, that that was the reason you had run away—'

'It wasn't.'

Nikolas grimaced. 'I can believe that now. But I have to admit that at the time I did not have such confidence. I had only your father's word—and the evidence of my own eyes—to convince me that you had no further use for my affections.'

'Oh, Nikolas!'

'You do believe me, don't you?'

'Yes, I believe you.'

'Because I have to tell you that after the lies Ariadne has been spreading about me my ego is sadly dented.'

'I believe you,' Paige said again, and this time when he bent to kiss her she wound her arms around his neck.

Hunger and sweet, sweet desire flowered inside her. Nikolas's lips and the damp heat he was generating filled her heart and her mind with an aching need that only he could assuage. His breath was warm in her mouth, his tongue touching and exploring all those dark and moist places that opened to his sensual caress. Her eyes closed, and she gave herself up to sensory pleasures, an involuntary moan escaping her when he released her mouth to seek the scented hollow of her throat.

Memories enveloped her, but they were good memories now, and only heightened her response to his urgent embrace. His hands spanned her shoulders briefly and then curved down the arching column of her spine, bringing her yielding body even closer to the powerful thrust of his. His hands cupped her bottom, lifting her against him, his fingers skimming the cleft that tightened almost automatically at his touch.

She was no innocent girl now, and when he eased one muscled thigh between her legs her eyes opened wide to see the hot passion in his face. His own need, stark and thrilling, darkened his eyes, burned like a torch in their depths, drove her to grab fistfuls of his hair and drag his mouth back to hers.

She wanted him, she thought dizzily. She'd always wanted him, and it was incredible to believe that that impossible dream was almost within reach...

'Hey, Paige—ooh, whoops!'

Sophie's eruption into the room was as unexpected as it was unwelcome and Paige felt an almost agonising pang of regret when Nikolas stifled a groan and slowly, but firmly, put her away from him.

There was an awkward moment's silence when Paige nurtured the faint hope that Sophie might show some discretion and walk out again. But she'd known it was an unlikely possibility. Her sister was far too curious to allow something so intriguing to go unchallenged, and when she propped her shoulder against the jamb Paige knew she was going to demand an explanation she didn't have.

'Does this mean we won't be leaving, after all?' Sophie asked, with her usual insensitivity, and Paige wanted to die with embarrassment.

'Sophie!' she exclaimed, hoping her sister would get the message, but before the younger girl could respond Nikolas's hand had looped around Paige's wrist.

'I take it you wouldn't have any objections?' he enquired, addressing himself to Sophie, but all Paige was aware of was his thumb rubbing sensuously against her palm.

Sophie blew out a breath. 'Are you serious?' she exclaimed, looking at her sister with a staggered expression. 'I mean—I thought—' She broke off in some confusion, and Paige enjoyed the experience of seeing her sister speechless for once.

'Yes? What did you think, Sophie?' Nikolas, too, appeared to be enjoying the moment, but Paige was not conceited enough to think that anything Sophie said would influence him one way or the other.

'Well, I—' Sophie gulped. 'Like—is this supposed to be some kind of joke or something?' She looked to her sister for support, but Paige was still too bemused by the feelings Nikolas was so effortlessly inspiring to have an answer for her. 'I thought you said Ariadne was going back to school.'

*'Me sinhorite!'* For a moment Nikolas was so disconcerted by this apparent *non sequitur* that he lapsed into his own language, and Sophie sighed in frustration.

'Paige said we were leaving,' she declared resentfully, staring at her sister. 'Didn't you, Paige? Well, are we or aren't we? I have a right to know.'

'Ah…' Nikolas recovered his composure before Paige could say anything, but instead of answering her he adopted a rather humorous expression. 'Well, Sophie, I would say that your question is a little—how shall I put it?—premature?'

*Premature!*

*Oh, God!*

With a feeling of complete devastation, Paige detached her hand from Nikolas's and put some space between them. She'd been such a fool, she thought painfully, avoiding his curious gaze. Why hadn't she seen what was happening? Why hadn't she realised that he had spoken in the past tense? He'd said he had fallen in love with her; that he'd *wanted* to marry her. Then, not now. Now all he wanted was satisfaction—a chance to prove to himself that she was still as vulnerable to him as she had ever been…

'Premature?' It was Sophie who was speaking again, and Paige wanted desperately to shut her up. 'What do you mean, premature? There didn't seem to be anything premature about the way you two were acting when—'

'Sophie!'

Paige was mortified, but Nikolas seemed to find Sophie's candour amusing. 'You're right,' he said as Paige started across the room to push her sister out of the door. He came after her, and although she attempted to resist he slipped his arm around her waist, successfully halting her in mid-flight. 'We had just begun to understand one another, hadn't we, *aghapita*?' he whispered. And, to her ignominy and Sophie's amazement, he bestowed a lingering kiss on her nape. 'For the first time in four years, we were being completely honest with one another.'

Paige drew a trembling breath. 'Is that what you call it?' she muttered in an undertone, but she couldn't prevent her automatic response to the heat of his body at her back.

'It will do for now,' he chided her softly. 'Stop fighting me, *mora*, or your sister will think you do not love me, after all.'

'Love you?' The words fell helplessly from Paige's lips, and, ignoring Sophie's stunned face, he turned her in his arms and lowered his mouth to hers.

'As I love you,' he conceded gently.

Paige quivered. 'You said—you said Sophie's question was premature—'

'And it was. I have not yet had the time to tell you how I feel; to ask you to do me the honour of becoming my wife.'

Paige's knees sagged, and now even Sophie found the naked emotion between them just too private to intrude upon.

'I guess we are staying,' she mumbled ruefully, backing out of the room, and wasn't really surprised when no one even noticed that she'd gone...

# EPILOGUE

PAIGE awakened to the sound of rain pattering against the deck above her head. The weather had broken at last, she thought ruefully, but she couldn't altogether say it mattered. Despite the fact that they had been cruising through the Ionian Islands and into the Adriatic, she and Nikolas had spent much of the past three weeks closeted in their state-room, and there was something intensely appealing about the intimacy the rain was creating.

She sighed contentedly. It was early yet and she knew she ought to close her eyes and go back to sleep again. But she couldn't resist turning her head, and the sight of Nikolas's dark head buried in the pillow beside her was an irresistible temptation. Although it was three weeks since they had stood together in the small church in Agios Petros and made their vows to one another, she still found it incredibly hard to believe that he was her husband; that he loved her just as much as she loved him, and that the mistakes of the past were just a painful memory.

She had long since forgiven her father for his part in their separation. It was terrible what the pressures of a failing business could do, she thought. She could only be grateful that he had brought her and Nikolas together in the first place, and she had come to bless her husband's subsequent desire for revenge for making their reunion possible.

Of course, she knew now that Nikolas would never have done anything to hurt her. Where she was concerned he was totally vulnerable, and even their closest relatives had been amazed at the feelings he didn't even try to hide.

After her experiences with Ariadne, Paige had been afraid that Nikolas's parents might object to their only son marrying an Englishwoman, particularly the Englishwoman who had apparently caused him such pain four years ago. But Elena and Constantine Petronides had been so relieved that their son was going to get married at last that their congratulations had been warmly sincere. They wanted a daughter-in-law; they wanted more grandchildren; and if Paige had suspected that they had any doubts about her suitability to be Nikolas's wife Eleni Petronides had quickly disposed of them. Ever since his earlier encounter with Paige, Nikolas had refused to consider the possibility of marrying anyone, and they had been unhappily convinced that their son was never going to achieve the kind of happiness his parents had shared.

His sisters, Oriana and Melina, had been less easy to win over. Although they were both married with children of their own, they loved their brother dearly and had perhaps been more aware than their parents of how Paige's apparent betrayal had affected him. But, gradually, they too had been forced to acknowledge that Nikolas had never been happier, and Melina, who had two little girls, had shown her approval by allowing them to join Sophie and Ariadne as Paige's bridesmaids at the wedding.

Paige allowed a sound of pure delight to escape her. It had been such a beautiful wedding, she thought, remembering how handsome Nikolas had looked with genuine pride. Aunt Ingrid had seemed totally bemused by the occasion, but she had happily agreed to stay on afterwards and keep an eye on both Sophie and Ariadne while Paige and Nikolas were on honeymoon.

Yanis was staying on the island, too, sharing the running of the Petronides corporation with Nikolas's father—who had been persuaded to come out of retirement for the weeks his son would be away. A situation which relieved Paige enormously. Aunt Ingrid was sweet, but Sophie could run rings around her, and Ariadne, who had been so relieved not to be sent back to school before the start of term in

September, had developed a totally unexpected attachment to the younger girl.

It had been agreed that both Sophie and Ariadne would board at school from the start of the autumn term: Ariadne at the convent she had previously attended, and Sophie at an English school in Athens. Both girls would spend weekends with their adoptive guardians, when possible, but Nikolas had no intention of leaving his new wife behind when business took him on trips about Europe and to the United States. Being permanently responsible for two teenagers would have prevented this.

In fact, both the girls had accepted the new arrangement without protest, and although Paige was sure the future wasn't all going to be such plain sailing—pardon the pun, she thought humorously—as long as she and Nikolas were together there was nothing they couldn't face.

But thinking about Nikolas had made her restless and she turned onto her side to gaze at her husband with mischievous eyes. He looked so comfortable, she thought, lying on his back, legs splayed, one arm above his head, the other at his side, an indication that even in sleep he trusted her completely.

Which was a dangerous thing to do, she thought whimsically, drawing the covers back from his waist to expose the whole length of his body to her possessive gaze. He was so appealing; so male, she acknowledged tremulously, not immune to the powerful strength of his torso or the sensual growth of dark hair that sprinkled his chest and arrowed down to the impressive cluster of curls that guarded his sex.

Her breath caught in her throat and, unable to stop herself, she spread her hand on his flat stomach. The muscles flinched beneath her fingers but his breathing didn't falter, and gaining confidence, Paige allowed her exploration to move lower. His sex lay within her reach now, lightly aroused and velvety soft to touch, as she knew, but when she attempted to enclose him within her grasp his sudden erection had her pulling back in surprise.

Yet she shouldn't have been surprised, she thought ruefully. She'd had plenty of experience to know how easy it was for her to bring him to an immediate state of arousal. But she'd thought he was asleep, and it was all the more daunting to find he was awake and watching her with lazily amused eyes.

'A little curiosity?' he asked mockingly. 'I hope I satisfied all your expectations.'

'Don't you always?' demanded Paige, stung into a defensive retaliation. And then, because she knew he was only teasing her, she pulled a face at him before bending her head to circle his navel with her tongue. 'I hope I've satisfied yours.'

'How could you doubt it?' said Nikolas, his voice a little less controlled now. And, as she allowed her tongue to trail lower, he added, 'I hope you realise what you're doing.'

'I think so,' said Paige, lifting her head to give him an impish grin. 'I'm just—waking you up, that's all. Don't they say that even Sleeping Beauty was awakened with a kiss?'

'Not there,' said Nikolas in a strangled voice, and, struggling up on his elbows, he managed to remove part of his anatomy from her caressing tongue. 'Come here,' he muttered, hauling her over him, and then groaned when she parted her legs so that the hot, moist core of her was cradling his sex.

'Let me,' she said, when he would have rolled her over, and, straddling him, she allowed him to invade her tight, wet sheath.

There was a delicious delight in knowing she was giving him pleasure and Paige moved slowly and sensuously over him until her own needs quickened her pace. Their release was almost simultaneous, and Nikolas did roll her over then

and buried his face in the scented hollow between her
breasts.

'Do you have any idea how much I love you?' he asked
huskily, his still shuddering body trembling in her arms,
and Paige felt a surge of love for him thicken in her throat.

'About as much as I love you?' she offered unsteadily,
but he pushed himself up from her and shook his head.

'And more,' he told her softly, a catch in his voice.
'These last two months have been the happiest time of my
life.'

'And mine,' said Paige, lifting a hand to shape his cheek,
allowing him to take her fingers into his mouth. 'We're so
lucky. Some people go through life and never find the one
person who is important to them.'

'And to think I nearly lost you,' agreed Nikolas, bringing
her palm to his lips. 'I was such a fool.'

'We both were,' said Paige, not allowing him to take all
the blame. 'You know, Daddy wasn't always so unscrupulous. I think he and my mother shared something special,
too, and when she died…' She sighed. 'Do you understand?'

'I'm trying to,' said Nikolas, nodding. 'I have to say that
at this moment I can only bless your father for bringing us
together in the first place. I think we can leave the rest. I'm
only sorry he never knew how much I love his daughter…'

# MILLS & BOON®

*Makes any time special*™

**Mills & Boon publish 29 new titles every month. Select from...**

Modern Romance™        Tender Romance™

Sensual Romance™

Medical Romance™  Historical Romance™

MAT2

# 4 FREE

## books and a surprise gift!

We would like to take this opportunity to thank you for reading this Mills & Boon® book by offering you the chance to take FOUR more specially selected titles from the Modern Romance™ series absolutely FREE! We're also making this offer to introduce you to the benefits of the Reader Service™—

- ★ FREE home delivery
- ★ FREE gifts and competitions
- ★ FREE monthly Newsletter
- ★ Exclusive Reader Service discounts
- ★ Books available before they're in the shops

Accepting these FREE books and gift places you under no obligation to buy, you may cancel at any time, even after receiving your free shipment. Simply complete your details below and return the entire page to the address below. *You don't even need a stamp!*

✂ **YES!** Please send me 4 free Modern Romance books and a surprise gift. I understand that unless you hear from me, I will receive 6 superb new titles every month for just £2.40 each, postage and packing free. I am under no obligation to purchase any books and may cancel my subscription at any time. The free books and gift will be mine to keep in any case.

P0ZEA

Ms/Mrs/Miss/Mr ...........................Initials...................................
BLOCK CAPITALS PLEASE

Surname ........................................................................................

Address ........................................................................................

........................................................................................................

.............................................................Postcode...........................

**Send this whole page to:**
**UK: FREEPOST CN81, Croydon, CR9 3WZ**
**EIRE: PO Box 4546, Kilcock, County Kildare (stamp required)**

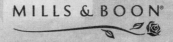